KNIGHTQUEEN

ORONIS KNIGHTS
BOOK 3

ANNA HACKETT

Knightqueen

Published by Anna Hackett

Copyright 2024 by Anna Hackett

Cover by Ana Cruz Arts

Edits by Tanya Saari

ISBN (ebook): 978-1-923134-15-7

ISBN (paperback): 978-1-923134-16-4

This book is a work of fiction. All names, characters, places and incidents are either the product of the author's imagination or are used fictitiously. Any resemblance to actual persons, events or places is coincidental. No part of this book may be reproduced, scanned, or distributed in any printed or electronic form.

WHAT READERS ARE SAYING ABOUT ANNA'S ACTION ROMANCE

Heart of Eon - Romantic Book of the Year (Ruby) winner 2020

Cyborg - PRISM Award Winner 2019

Edge of Eon and Mission: Her Protection - Romantic Book of the Year (Ruby) finalists 2019

Unfathomed and Unmapped - Romantic Book of the Year (Ruby) finalists 2018

Unexplored – Romantic Book of the Year (Ruby) Novella Winner 2017

Return to Dark Earth – One of Library Journal's Best E-Original Books for 2015 and two-time SFR Galaxy Awards winner

At Star's End – One of Library Journal's Best E-Original Romances for 2014

The Phoenix Adventures – SFR Galaxy Award Winner for Most Fun New Series and "Why Isn't This a Movie?" Series

Beneath a Trojan Moon – SFR Galaxy Award Winner and RWAus Ella Award Winner

Hell Squad – SFR Galaxy Award for best Post-Apocalypse for Readers who don't like Post-Apocalypse

"Like Indiana Jones meets Star Wars. A treasure hunt with a steamy romance." – SFF Dragon, review of *Among Galactic Ruins*

"Action, danger, aliens, romance – yup, it's another great book from Anna Hackett!" – Book Gannet Reviews, review of *Hell Squad: Marcus*

Sign up for my VIP mailing list and get your *free box set* containing three action-packed romances.

Visit here to get started: www.annahackett.com

CHAPTER ONE

She was being hunted.

Knightqueen Carys crouched in the shadows behind a large boulder. Down here, at the bottom of the huge ravine, the ground was littered with broken rocks, and the shadows were deep and dark.

She looked up at the sheer walls of rock that rose high above her. She had no idea what planet she was on, but so far, all she'd seen were jagged mountains and cavernous ravines.

The deep snort of a beast made her pulse pick up. She breathed out slowly, her muscles tense. The sharp scrape of claws on rock caught her ear.

She might be the Knightqueen, the ruler of the Oronis people, but she was also a trained knight. Her body contained combat implants that made her a skilled fighter.

She pulled a face. She couldn't access her implants completely at the moment. Her captors had pumped her full of drugs to block her abilities.

But now that she was free, she was slowly regaining access to some of her implants.

She might be filthy and exhausted, and wearing the tatters of what had once been a grand, gold ballgown, her bare feet scraped and bloody, but that didn't matter. She was an Oronis knight to the core. Her enemy would pay for abducting her.

There was a skitter of rocks, and Carys quickly darted over to the next boulder.

The most important thing, though, was that she wasn't alone.

She glanced at the faint, gold glow of the band around her wrist. The dura-binding ran along the rocks, disappearing into the darkness. A bond of pure energy that no one could break.

Focus on the creature, Carys. She lifted her gaze. *Come on, beastie. Show yourself.*

A low growl raised the hairs on the back of her neck.

With a speed that shocked her, the beast leaped onto the boulder in front of her, lifted its head, and roared.

It had scaly, gray skin, two powerful back legs, smaller front legs, and a thick, long tail studded with spikes. There were no eyes that she could see but she knew it was looking at her. It opened its mouth, revealing sharp fangs. Drool dripped on the rocks by her feet.

Carys steeled herself and raised her hands. Energy flowed through her veins. It was weaker than it should be, but she'd make sure it was enough.

Pushing, she felt the flow increase, warm and electrifying. Her *oralite* nano-implant kicked in, channeling the energy, a ball of blue light forming between her palms.

She threw the energy ball.

The monster dodged. The blue energy clipped it and it snarled, tail whipping behind it.

More energy pulsed, filling her body. Her anger joined it. She'd been snatched violently from her very own ball in her own palace. She'd been forcibly taken from her planet, Oron, and treated like an animal. Caged, beaten, locked in a prison.

Her enemy, the Gek'Dragar, had done this. Her jaw tightened. They would pay.

She knew they were building up to an attack. They wouldn't stay in their own space long. No, soon, they'd come for Oron.

There was *no way* she'd let that happen. It was her duty to protect her people.

She would *not* let the Gek'Dragar win.

Carys threw out her arms and tried to form her armor. She felt the weakest pulse of energy, then nothing.

By the coward's bones. Instead, she focused on a weapon.

The sword formed in her hand, energy swirling, growing into existence. She gripped the hilt as the blade glowed blue.

The monster shook its head, its eye-less face fixated on her.

"Come on, then." She lifted the sword horizontally over her head. She'd trained with the blade since she could walk.

The creature roared, more drool dripping off its huge fangs onto the rocks below, and nothing but mindless rage radiated off it.

It leaped, its powerful, scaled body sailing through the air.

Carys' heart thudded hard. *Wait. Wait.*

Then a large figure leaped in from the left, his big body a blur.

Knightguard Thorsten Carahan soared through the air. He held a giant, blue broadsword in his hands.

Her pulse leaped as she watched him. He used his strength and momentum to drive the sword into the beast's body.

Carys dived and rolled, conscious of the dura-binding linking her to her knightguard. They'd lengthened it to give them room to maneuver, but she didn't want to get tangled up.

Sten and the monster crashed to the ground. He pulled his sword free of the animal's hide, and ugly, black blood dripped onto the rocks. He stabbed it again, ensuring it was dead.

"Carys."

The low rumble of his voice moved through her and she fought back a shiver. She closed the distance between them. "I'm fine. I play the bait very well, I think."

Sten made an unhappy sound. She knew every scowl, every look, and every sound that her knightguard made. He'd been her personal guard for over a decade. He'd protected her without question. He'd trained for it all his life.

She'd never ever questioned his ability, or his loyalty.

He glanced her way. His brown hair was short, and his features rugged. One cheek was covered in scars he'd gotten protecting her. No one would accuse Sten of being handsome, and if they did, he'd probably hit them.

No, Sten was pure strength and rugged power.

"I still can't make my armor," she said.

"Me neither." He wore his own ripped, dirty black clothing he'd been wearing at the ball. His shirt had several tears, bronze skin showing through.

And he still made her breath stutter.

Alone, lost on an alien planet, it was just the two of them.

There was no protocol, palace workers, other knights, or the thousands of meetings and gatherings she attended as queen to keep them locked in their roles of knightqueen and knightguard.

It made it harder for her to hide her feelings.

Suddenly, several small creatures skittered over the rocks.

Oh, no. The beasts down here never stopped. These ones had lots of legs, and hard bodies, but their fangs looked just as sharp.

She tensed. "Sten."

"I see them."

He swiveled, and they pressed their backs together. Carys lifted her sword.

"Wait for them," he said. "Wait."

Carys waved her sword, a wash of blue light lighting the area around them.

The small creatures reared, spikes appearing on their legs.

"Go!" Sten roared.

They charged together, blades swinging and slashing.

She gritted her teeth, her sword cutting through hard shells and sharp claws. Black blood splashed the rocks.

Whirling, she and Sten moved with power and precision. He threw an energy ball.

Several more alien creatures came up over the rocks. Her jaw tightened. She'd be no one's meal today.

She slashed at more creatures, then formed another energy ball and tossed it into a crowd of the beasts.

"Sten." She ran in his direction.

It was like he read her mind. He bent forward and she rolled over his back and sent out a wave of energy. It hit the creatures, the powerful blast tossing their bodies into the air.

The last few alien monsters retreated, skittering back into the shadows.

Quiet fell. All Carys could hear was her and Sten's harsh breathing.

She dissolved her sword. Sten waited another beat, before dissolving his, as well.

He straightened and scanned the area.

She studied his rugged face, and the scars that slashed down one cheek.

He'd gotten them protecting her when she'd been a teenager. They'd been attacked by a vicious creature intent on assassinating her. Not once had he given up, or slackened from his duty, even when he'd been injured and in pain.

Suddenly, tiredness hit. Carys was so sore, weary, and hungry. They'd been held captive for days, and been carted halfway across the quadrant to...wherever they were. The entire time she'd worried about Oron and her people.

When they'd escaped the Gek'Dragar prison, she'd been filled with hope. But after a day of travelling through these beast-infested ravines, fighting for their lives, she was tired.

Sagging, she dropped onto a rock.

"Carys." Sten knelt in front of her and cupped her face.

"I just need a minute. I'll be fine."

She was always fine. She had to be. Her people wanted to see strength and grace in their queen.

Not a woman who often felt alone. A woman who keenly felt the weight of her people's safety weighing on her. There were always vital decisions to make, political alliances to navigate, and enemies waiting for a moment of weakness.

"You're exhausted," he said.

She met green eyes she knew so well. "So are you."

His callused thumbs moved on her cheeks, and she hid the shiver of pleasure that ran down her spine.

Then a fierce frown crossed his face. He leaned down and picked up one of her feet in his hands. He made one of his unhappy sounds. Her skin was torn and bleeding.

"The bindings came off," she said.

He'd wrapped her bare feet the best he could in shreds of his shirt.

"It's fine, Sten."

"No, it's not," he growled.

"They'll heal." Another benefit of their combat implants was that they helped their wounds heal faster.

"But your healing rate is still slow after the drugs the Gek'Dragar gave us." His scowl turned savage. "Another thing I will ensure they pay for."

She touched his wrist. His skin was warm. Back in the palace, they rarely touched. But out here, everything was different. "First, we focus on escaping. There will be time for vengeance."

His serious gaze bored into hers. "Nothing is more important than your safety." He dragged in a breath. "You need food and rest. Not to be fighting these infernal beasts."

She reached up and touched his jaw. "Sten."

Turbulent green eyes met hers.

"I'm with you, so I'm fine," she said.

His face was so solemn, and her heart squeezed. She loved those rugged features.

She loved him.

Her chest squeezed. Not that he knew it. He'd be horrified to hear it. He didn't see her as a woman, just as his queen, his duty.

She was destined to pine for a man who didn't see her the same way.

At balls and events, men from around the quadrant praised her beauty. But the one man she wanted most, didn't see her that way.

Oh, he knew her—what she liked, what she disliked, what made her mad, what made her happy. But he didn't see a sensual woman.

He only saw her crown, the person he had to protect.

Sten cocked his head. "What are you thinking about?"

Sometimes he knew her too well. "Getting out of here."

Then he glanced past her, looking down the ravine. He cocked his head, gaze narrowing.

"What is it?" she asked.

"Someone's coming." He scooped her up into his arms.

"You should unfasten the dura-binding," she said. "We'll be able to move more easily."

"No." He'd already refused many times before, worried the Gek'Dragar would capture them again.

He'd slipped the bond on when they'd been attacked in the palace on Oron. It couldn't be removed by anyone else without killing both of them. It was why the Gek'-Dragar had taken him, as well.

He moved along the cliff wall, and found a crack large enough for them to squeeze into. They pushed into the tight space, and he quickly stacked some rocks in front of them, then turned to her.

They were pressed together, his arms wrapped around her. She felt his hot breath on her neck and closed her eyes. He felt so big, so strong.

Then, sounds echoed in the ravine. Heavy footsteps and deep voices.

Her breath hitched.

Through a small crack in the rocks, she saw a Gek'-Dragar soldier step into view.

CHAPTER TWO

By the coward's bones.

Seeing the large form of the enemy made Sten Carahan want to charge out and kill.

The Gek'Dragar was tall, with powerful legs and broad shoulders. It was humanoid, except for the long, scaled tail behind it. A high-tech suit covered most of its body, but pale-gray, scaled skin showed on its neck and face. Two ridges ran along its cheeks, and four bony horns—two on each side—swept back from its face. The soldier had black hair that almost touched its shoulders, and its green eyes glowed in the gloom.

Sten's jaw was so tight it ached. They'd dared to take the knightqueen. They'd invaded Oron, attacked the palace, and stolen her away.

He'd been forced to watch them hurt her and lock her up.

His hands balled into fists. It had been pure instinct to link them with a dura-binding during the attack.

It meant the Gek'Dragar had been forced to take him with them.

They hadn't been happy. He'd taken several beatings and still had the bruises.

At least he was with her. And he would get her home.

He tightened his hold on her body. She was staying still and watchful.

Holding her like this…it wasn't something he usually did back on Oron. Over the years, he'd memorized how she looked, how she walked, every nuance of her beautiful features. In his darkest fantasies—ones he tried to keep ruthlessly locked down—he'd imagined touching her.

He breathed her in. Yes, they were both dirty, but his enhanced senses could still pull out her scent. It always made him think of sun-kissed honey.

You're the head of her knightguard.

His jaw worked. He had no right to touch her. He was older, scarred, her guard. That was it.

I am Knightguard Thorsten Carahan. It is my duty to protect my queen. I am her sword, her shield, and her devoted servant.

He repeated his private vow a few more times.

The Gek'Dragar soldiers marched past their hiding place. But it was clear they were searching for them.

Sten and Carys had escaped their rocky prison built in the mountains here. There had been some sort of commotion at the prison, and they'd escaped in the chaos.

As they'd climbed down into the deep ravine, he'd heard the explosion that had destroyed the prison. It had provided the perfect distraction for him to get Carys far away from the Gek'Dragar.

Now, they were stuck on an unknown alien planet.

Alone.

The first thing they needed was food, and a safe place to rest. He knew that Carys was tired, and even though they had combat implants, they still weren't functioning at full capacity. He ground his teeth together. The Gek'-Dragar had shot them full of drugs that had left them unable to use their implants.

But it was wearing off. Soon, they'd be at full capacity again.

Still, even their tech couldn't keep them upright for days on end. They needed rest. Carys' feet were scratched up badly, and he hated seeing her golden skin damaged. He hated more that it wasn't healing like it should.

Sten leaned closer to the opening. He listened, using his enhanced hearing.

The Gek'Dragar were gone.

"Come on." He moved the rocks carefully, then helped her out.

She looked as graceful as ever, even in her tattered and torn dress. Days ago, she'd asked him to tear the long skirt shorter to give her more movement.

She was tall and slender, like a dancer. Her white-blonde hair was dirty and tangled, but she still looked like a queen. Her eyes were a brilliant gold.

He took her hand, loving the way her elegant fingers tangled with his. He pulled her in the opposite direction to the Gek'Dragar. They moved swiftly along the bottom of the ravine.

He hated it down here. This planet had too many wild beasts that bred and lived in the shadows. From what he could tell, there was something unnatural about them. They were twisted and mutated.

He looked up. There was nothing around them but sheer cliffs that seemed never-ending, reaching for the sky.

Then his gaze snagged on something. About halfway up the cliff face, a broken bridge dangled high above. And on one side, he spotted stone dwellings cut into the cliffside.

"This way." He walked until he found a narrow, steep path that led up the cliff. "We're going up."

She nodded. "Where are we going exactly?"

"There's some sort of dwelling cut into the rocks above. Maybe an old village."

She arched her neck and looked up. "It looks abandoned."

"If there's shelter, we can rest there." He just hoped there were no *gul*-vexed beasts up there. He was pretty sure the creatures stuck to the ravines, but he wasn't taking any chances.

Sten started up the steep path, keeping one hand pressed to the rock face. In places, the path was crumbled and narrow. They reached a spot where the path deteriorated away, leaving a wide gap.

He leaped over it. He turned and held out a hand. Carys easily jumped across the gap, bumping into him.

"Okay?" he asked.

"Yes. Lead on."

They kept moving, but eventually the path petered out. It stopped at a sheer face of dark rock.

"What now?" She sounded so tired.

Sten spun. "Hop on my back."

"What?"

"Come on, Carys. It's getting dark." He waved at his back. He had no idea what other creatures might come out at night. "We need to scale this cliff before we lose the remaining light."

There was a pause, then she leaped onto his back.

He froze for a second and closed his eyes. The knightqueen's long legs were wrapped around his waist. She was pressed against his back.

For a second, all he could do was feel.

Guilt punched him in the gut. She was his queen. He was supposed to be getting her to safety not reacting to her body.

He shook his head, then faced the cliff wall. He pressed a hand into a crack, then launched himself upward.

He needed to focus on his job, and not how soft and warm she felt.

Sten climbed. Her weight barely added anything. He'd trained with packs heavier than her. She held tight and didn't move or complain as he worked his way up the cliff.

He gripped a crack and moved to haul himself up.

The rock crumbled away. He lost his grip on his right hand, his body sliding downward.

Carys gasped.

With his left hand, Sten clung hard, his arm muscles straining. "It's...okay." He found a ledge with his right hand and evened his body out.

"I can climb myself—"

"No." The thought of her clinging to the rock face had sweat breaking out on his forehead. "We're almost there."

He hauled his body up and searched for his next handhold.

Finally, he climbed over the edge into the ruins. *Thank the knights.*

He set Carys down and wiped the sweat off his face. She straightened, staring at the silent, dusty rock-cut dwellings.

A quick scan told him that there was no one here. At least no one living and breathing.

"This was once someone's home." She walked to the closest carved building, stepping through a doorway. Inside, some rotting furniture lay tipped over and abandoned, and rubble had crumbled off the walls and ceilings. She bent down and picked up a rotting piece of fabric. The color had long since faded.

The sunlight was nearly gone, and Sten used his energy to create blue light on his palm. They used it to search the rest of the village.

The dwellings were all empty.

"The Gek'Dragar are responsible for this." Anger coated Carys' voice. "I know it. Whoever lived here, the Gek'Dragar forced them out."

"Yeah, the *guls* have a lot to answer for." Something moved in the shadows and Sten spotted a small lizard.

Quickly, he chased it, and gripped the small creature. It wriggled, but he quickly twisted its neck.

"Sten!"

"It's food." He scanned the creature with his implant. It was fine to eat and had a high protein content.

Carys' nose wrinkled. "I'm not eating it raw."

"Yes, my queen." He took her arm, and led her into the least ruined building carved into the cliff. At the back, he saw a vine growing over one wall. It was laden with white fruit. A quick scan told him the fruit was edible as well. He plucked several off the vine.

Carys ducked into an adjoining room. "Sten, in here."

He followed her and saw where water trickled down the wall, pooling in a basin carved into the rock. He scanned the water. Potable. Something else to thank the knights of old for. A quick circle of the room, and he found a carved bowl made of some type of wood. That meant there might be trees on this planet somewhere, although he was yet to see any. He rinsed the bowl out, and filled it with water.

When he handed it to her, she drank greedily. He watched her graceful neck, his gut tightening. A droplet of water escaped, sliding down her neck. He swallowed. He had the sudden urge to lean forward and lap at that drop. At her skin.

Gul. He made himself look away.

He needed to find his control. His hand flexed. He was usually very good at not letting himself notice how beautiful his knightqueen was.

He'd had years of practice.

I am Knightguard Thorsten Carahan. It is my duty to protect my queen. I am her sword, her shield, and her devoted servant.

"Come on, let's find somewhere to rest for the night." He led her back into the main room of the house. He found a small table that was kicked over on its side, and righted it, setting their food down. He found a few other things buried in the rubble.

There was a candle made from some sort of slow-burning wax. He lit it, and it gave the room a flickering glow. Next, he pulled up some netting, and realized it was a hammock. He dusted it off and affixed it to the wall, then he tested it with his weight.

"It's stable."

He crouched down on the ground, then used a burst of energy to cook the lizard.

Carys sat down beside him. She pulled a face as he used a knife to slice the cooked creature, but she took a hunk of the lizard meat. He watched her gingerly test it.

"I'd give anything for some *berrigian* broth right now," she said.

A popular meal on Oron, it was made from a flavorful vegetable, and he knew it was one of her favorites.

"As soon as we get home."

She shot him a small smile that made his chest tighten. "And you'd want a thick *brod* steak."

She named his favorite meat. "You know me too well."

"I do."

Quietly, they ate the fruit and meat, taking sips of

water in between. The silence was comfortable and familiar.

They'd spent a lot of time together since he'd become her guard.

She'd been a young, bubbly, seventeen-year-old, and already so amazingly beautiful, when he'd been assigned to her protection detail.

It had been an honor to protect the life of the knight-princess.

Then the Gek'Dragar had organized the assassination of her parents. They'd tried to kill her, as well, but Sten had stopped that attack. He reached up and stroked the scars on his cheek.

"I'm surprisingly full." She leaned back against the wall.

The candlelight made her pale skin look a deeper gold. By the stars, she was beautiful.

He cleared his throat. "Feet now."

She huffed out a breath, but rested her feet in his lap. He soaked some fabric in water and then started cleaning her feet. They were long, narrow, and elegant. There was gold color on her toenails.

"I wonder what this planet is called," she said. "And what happened to all the inhabitants."

Sten remained silent. As far as he could tell, they were in Gek'Dragar space. The enemy had killed the locals, or driven them out. He had no idea if there were any left.

It was what the Gek'Dragar did.

They were selfish, only thinking of the needs of their

own species. They thrived on combat, and hated any sort of harmony.

They took whatever they wanted with no regard to the consequences.

His jaw tightened. They wouldn't take Carys again. He wouldn't allow it.

"We need a plan, Sten."

"You need to rest." While she slept, he'd stand guard and make sure no one snuck up on them. "Tomorrow, the first thing we need to do is put more distance between us and the Gek'Dragar. We'll search for a local village or settlement. If we're lucky, we might find a communications device. We need to get a message to Oron."

She nibbled her lip. "The Gek'Dragar are looking for us."

"They are. But Knightmaster Ashtin and the entire Knightforce will be working to find you." Sten called Knightmaster Ashtin Caydor a friend. The man was a dedicated knight, and Sten knew Ashtin would do everything in his power to bring the queen home.

Sten finished with her feet, and let himself have one last stroke of her heel before he gave them a tap.

As she pulled them out of his lap, they brushed his thigh, and he stifled a curse. His cock was not listening to all his reasons why he had to keep his feelings locked down.

Once they were back on Oron, it would be fine. Things would go back to normal.

He saw Carys' eyelids droop, and then she shivered. The temperature was dropping, now that the sun was gone.

"Time to sleep," he ordered.

With a slow nod, she climbed into the hammock. It rocked gently. Sten shifted to lean his head back against the wall.

"Sten?"

"Yeah."

"Will you...lie with me? It's cold, and I don't want to be alone."

He froze. It wasn't right, and his control didn't need any more testing. "I don't think—"

"Please?"

She was his queen. He could never say no to her.

I am Knightguard Thorsten Carahan. It is my duty to protect my queen. I am her sword, her shield, and her devoted servant.

He climbed into the hammock, and it rocked more this time, as he settled his weight into it. She instantly curled into his body. She was half lying on top of him, since he took up most of the space.

As they swayed, she pressed a hand to his chest. She snuggled in and let out a sigh. "You're so warm."

And her skin was chilled. He shifted his arms around her. By the stars, she felt nice. Soft. Feminine.

She nuzzled her cheek against his chest, and he closed his eyes. Moments later, he sensed when she fell asleep.

I will keep you safe. I will get you off this planet. He vowed it.

She shifted again, her thigh sliding over his.

His cock hardened.

Sten mentally cursed himself, staring up at the rocky

ceiling above. She was over ten years younger than him. She was his queen, and he was nothing. He was the simple son of a farmer. He was her guard, and it was his duty to keep her safe.

Jaw tight, he forced himself to find some control. But he still held her tight.

CHAPTER THREE

Mmm. It was nice to wake up warm and cozy.

It felt like so long since she'd felt like that.

Then Carys felt a hand on her bottom, squeezing gently. Her eyes snapped open.

She'd *never* had that experience before.

She'd never shared her bed with anyone.

Oh, stars. She blinked. She was sprawled over Sten, and he had one brawny arm wrapped around her. If he woke and found out he was cupping her ass possessively, he'd be horrified.

Her pulse fluttered, sensation moving through her belly. This felt so good. She'd wanted this so much. To be close to his big, scarred body. His solid, secure strength.

Sten was her rock.

He was the foundation she could always trust.

She let her gaze run over his face. She liked watching him sleep. He didn't look any softer or more relaxed, and she could take in his strong jaw and nose without him knowing. And the scars on the left side of his cheek.

KNIGHTQUEEN

Her chest squeezed. She'd been terrified when the vicious alien *nelok* had attacked. But he'd fought it off as it had tried desperately to get to her, and rip her to shreds.

They'd been ambushed on a ride outside of Aravena, the capital city of Oron. Sten had fought the *nelok* and found a cave for them to take shelter in. He'd kept fighting the creature off, even after it had clawed him badly. He'd eventually killed it with his bare hands.

Afterward, when they'd returned to the castle, he'd held her when she sobbed for her murdered parents.

She itched to reach out and touch his short brown hair. Most Oronis had white-blonde or black hair, and were tall and lean. But not Sten. He was big and brawny, with brown hair. He looked more like their allies, the Eon warriors.

Losing the battle, she reached out and gently touched his hair. In his sleep, he sighed and pulled her closer. The warmth of his body soaked into hers, lighting up several places inside her.

Carys closed her eyes. He was her knightguard. She was just a job to him.

She eased away and slipped off the hammock, savoring the final feel of his fingers on her skin.

As soon as she moved, he woke instantly.

"Are you all right, my queen?" His voice sounded like gravel.

She smiled. "I'm fine."

"Good." He sat up, then glared as the hammock rocked beneath him.

She hid her smile.

He stretched. "Do you want more fruit? Once we eat, we need to decide which direction to head."

She held up her wrist and pointed at the glowing binding joining them. "It'll be easier for us to travel without the dura-binding."

A muscle in his jaw ticked.

"We're heading away from the Gek'Dragar, Sten. If need be, you can slap it back into place."

He stared at her, and she knew he was weighing the odds.

She drew herself up and used her best "queen" tone. "Sten."

"Fine." He touched the band on his wrist, tapping out a sequence. A second later, the strands of gold winked out like they'd never even existed.

And just like that, she missed it. She missed being tied to him.

Shaking off the feeling of loss, Carys freshened up the best she could. She splashed some water on her face and finger-combed her hair.

She missed the palace. She missed her huge bathroom with its large tub that was like a pool, and her generous shower.

You'll get home.

She sat and nabbed one of the white fruits off the table. She bit into it, enjoying the sweet juice. She saw Sten wander outside their shelter, moving to the edge of the cliff. He looked every bit the Oronis knight. His thick, muscular thighs were almost the size of her waist, and those wide shoulders looked like they could carry any weight. As she watched him, those shoulders tensed.

Her throat was tight as she joined him. "What have you seen?"

"Gek'Dragar." His mouth was a flat line. "Look."

In the distance, a ship made of brown metal was flying in a clear search pattern, and several small drones were zipping through the air nearby.

A mix of fear and anger twisted inside her. "They're looking for us."

He nodded. "We'll go the other way. It's the best option anyway." He pointed.

In the distance she saw the glint of aqua blue. Her chest lifted. The ocean. Her gaze narrowed. She also could make out a plume of smoke. She shaded her eyes, but it was too far away for her to see clearly.

"Is that a settlement?"

"I think so."

Hope soared. "Then let's go."

"Your feet—"

"They healed a little while we were sleeping." She touched his arm and squeezed. "My scratched feet are the least of our worries." She glanced back toward the ocean.

There were a lot of menacing mountain peaks between them and their destination.

It wouldn't be an easy trek, especially barefoot. She lifted her chin. But she would do it. She was the knightqueen.

Sten searched through some of the other ruined buildings. He found an old leather pack and several bottles that he filled with water. He tucked the bottles and some of the fruit inside the pack.

Then he swung it on his shoulders. "Time to go."

Soon, they set off down a rocky path, heading away from the Gek'Dragar search patrol.

"I wonder what the people who lived here were like," she said. "What they did?"

"I suspect they were miners." He pointed across the ravine.

On the other side of the canyon, a round mine entrance was etched into the cliff face. It was closed off with a metal door. As she scanned down the valley, she saw other mine entrances dotted on the mountainside.

Sympathy washed through her. Clearly whatever these people had mined, the Gek'Dragar had wanted it.

As they moved down into the valley, the sun slowly rose overhead. Carys spotted some agile, long-limbed animals climbing the cliffs above with ease. They had sturdy hooves and shaggy fur on their bodies. She blew out a breath. She wished climbing was as easy for her. Her thigh muscles were already burning and her feet were throbbing.

She trained daily at home on Oron, but most of her days were filled with meetings with dignitaries or visits in the city. Strenuous hiking in dangerous terrain wasn't something she did often.

It didn't appear to bother Sten. As he moved ahead of her, never once slowing down or showing any strain, she pulled a face at his back. Sten hiked like he could do it for days on end.

Soon, the morning chill was gone, and she was warm, sweat running down her spine.

She tested her implants, but her connection to her

oralite still wasn't fully functional. Without the extra boost it gave her, she had to admit she was reaching the end of her limits.

Sure enough, a moment later, she stumbled. Sten whipped around fast and caught her.

"Careful."

"Sorry."

He frowned at her. "You're tired."

She let out a short laugh. "Can you blame me?"

"No. Sit." He helped her over to a rock.

She dropped down heavily, and Sten crouched beside her. He handed her a piece of fruit.

Her back was sore, her legs were sore, her feet were sore. Everything was sore. Dully, she bit into the fruit.

"You're in pain," he said.

"I'm just stiff."

She saw something in his gaze, then he moved behind her. His big hands clamped on her shoulders, and he started to knead her muscles.

"*Oh*." Pleasure shimmered through her. Not only at the massage, but also because Sten was touching her. She moaned.

His hands stilled.

"Don't stop," she said.

He resumed massaging her sore muscles. "Once we have full access to our *oralite*, it'll heal you."

She made a humming sound. His strong fingers hit a tender spot. "Oh, Sten. That feels so good."

He snatched his hands back and turned away. "That should help."

Carys felt like he'd hit her. *Stars, did he hate touching her that much?* A ball of pain grew in her gut.

"We should keep moving," he said gruffly.

With a sigh, she heaved herself up. "Onward."

They trekked on in silence.

STEN STOPPED, studying the old bridge across the canyon.

It was narrow and old, and frayed in places. It looked like it had been abandoned for a long time.

Frowning, he moved gingerly onto the bridge, testing its strength.

He stopped partway across, noting that there were several steel cables reinforcing it. He looked back over his shoulder and waved.

Carys moved out of the shadows on the other side of the crevasse and stepped onto the bridge.

He turned and continued on to the other side. There was a yawning opening in the rock. He could see light at the end of the tunnel somewhere. It clearly led through to the other side of this hill.

He'd noted that this entire mountain range was riddled with tunnels and mines, so he hoped they could continue to find shortcuts through them.

Carys was halfway across the bridge when she froze and looked up.

His pulse tripped, and suddenly, he heard the *whirr*.

A drone was coming.

"Hurry!" he yelled.

She picked up speed, pumping her arms. The sound of the drone echoed off the rock walls, getting louder.

She wasn't going to make it.

If the drone spotted her, the Gek'Dragar would descend on their location.

Carys clearly decided the same thing. She stopped and met his gaze.

"Carys," he murmured.

Then she gripped the railing of the rope bridge, and leaped over the side.

Sten's heart tried to burst from his chest. Her dress flapped as she gracefully fell, then arrowed her body in under the bridge. She clung to the bottom of it, pulling herself into a tight ball.

His heart thundered in his ears. It was hard to spot her, even when you knew exactly where to look.

Sten pushed his back against the rock in the tunnel, panic still drilling into his heart. Seeing her leap off the bridge, out over the ravine...

He crouched, and drew in a shaky breath.

The drone flew into view. It was made of brown metal, lights blinking along the sides. It was roughly spherical, with four short arms at the front.

It was definitely Gek'Dragar tech.

It slowed, flying over the bridge.

Move on. Move on.

The drone hovered for a second and Sten tensed. He flexed his hand, ready to attack.

If it spotted Carys...

Then, the machine flew on. Sten released a breath and made himself wait, which was agony. Carys was hanging over the *gul*-vexed ravine, clinging to the bridge. His muscles quivered.

Finally, the sound of the drone faded.

He leaped up. "*Carys.*" He ran onto the bridge.

She pulled herself over, flashing her bare legs at him.

He grabbed her hands.

"I'm fine," she said.

Suddenly, the whine of the drone returned.

He cursed. "Come on. *Fast.*"

They sprinted along the bridge. They barely reached the other side when he pulled her into the tunnel. He pressed her to the wall, covering her body with his.

A second later, the drone whizzed past. This time, it didn't slow down.

Sten let out a breath. "Are you all right?"

"Yes. I just really want *off* this *gul*-cursed planet."

"Me too." Suddenly, he realized he was plastered against her, her breasts pressed to his chest. His hands dug into her slim hips.

He stepped back hastily, his body instantly missing the feel of her.

She straightened, dusting off her skirt. "Let's go."

They moved through the tunnel. It wasn't long, and a few minutes later, they came out in a small, bowl-shaped valley, nestled amongst the mountains.

Carys gasped. "It's beautiful."

Lush greenery grew everywhere, nothing like the desolate, rocky bases of the ravines they'd been in.

Sten scanned for any danger, staying close to Carys.

"Sten." Her face lit up. "I can hear water."

She rushed ahead, pushing through the bushes. Muttering a curse, he charged in front of her, clearing the way, and holding the branches back.

A second later, they stepped out by a small, burbling pool. Kneeling beside it, Sten activated his implant and scanned it.

"The water's safe."

"Thank the stars." She dropped down and scooped up several handfuls to drink.

Sten cupped his hand and drank himself. Then he washed his face and hands.

"I want to bathe," she said.

He wasn't surprised. He knew it was a favorite pastime of Carys'. Her maids always talked about just how long their queen liked to soak in her tub. He rose and nodded. "I'll keep watch. Don't take too long."

She gave him a smile.

He strode back into the vegetation. A cute, fluffy animal popped out on a branch and looked at him. It ruffled its fur and cooed at him. He scowled back at it.

At least there was no sign of the Gek'Dragar, or the monsters that bred in the ravines. This valley seemed like a small paradise.

The splashing water behind him made him think of golden skin.

Wet golden skin.

His jaw locked.

You're her knightguard.

He wasn't sure when thoughts of her had started invading his dreams. Years ago. Not when she'd been a girl. No, it had started after he realized she'd grown into a woman. A smart, sensual woman. For him, there was no one more beautiful than Carys.

But her beauty was more than her fine features and starlight hair. It was her goodness, her kindness, and her sense of fairness.

He released a breath. He was just a lowly guard, and she was the queen. She was beautiful, smart, and kind. He was none of those things.

Then he heard her gasp and cry out.

Without thinking, Sten spun and charged through the bushes at high speed.

He found her standing waist-deep in the water, and splashed in, clothes and all, then grabbed her.

"What's wrong?" Blood was pounding through his veins as he looked for danger.

"Um..."

He looked down. Her face was fresh and clean, with droplets clinging to her long eyelashes. Her hair looked shades darker when it was damp, and it clung to her head and shoulders.

"Carys?"

"It was a fish. It touched my foot. It didn't hurt me."

It took him a second. "A fish? You're not in danger?"

Her lips twitched. "No."

That's when he realized the full curves of her breasts were pressed to his chest. And she was naked.

He knew he should let her go, but his arms wouldn't obey. She was warm and wet, with the right amount of gentle curves. She was tall and slim, toned from training, but there was no doubting she was a woman. His gaze dropped to her lips.

He heard her breathing hitch. "Sten?"

His muscles tensed and he quickly took a step back.

His boot hit something slippery, and he swayed. They both grabbed at each other.

And one of Sten's palms closed around her breast.

He froze. He couldn't move, couldn't think.

Her lips parted, then she pushed into his hand. His fingers flexed and his cock lengthened, pushing against his trousers. Her eyes widened, and he knew she felt it.

Before he could stop himself, he stroked the curve of her breast. A small, husky sound escaped her lips and her nipple beaded.

"Sten," she breathed, color filling her cheeks.

It snapped him out of the moment.

He released her and staggered backward. Desire rode him hard, making his movements jerky.

"Call me if you need me," he said stiffly.

He tried not to look at her, or her breasts, flat belly, and long legs. But he couldn't help getting that one glimpse of those pink nipples, both hard nubs.

As he stomped out of the water, he tried to will his cock under control. But desire was hot and scorching his veins.

Out of sight, he pressed his back to a tree.

"She's your queen. You're stuck on a dangerous planet, fighting for survival." He pressed his palm to his cock and groaned.

It took him a while, but he slowly battled the desire

down. He dragged in some ragged breaths and managed to get a lock on his feelings. He shoved them down deep, then released a hard breath.

He wondered what would kill him first—the planet, or his need for Carys.

CHAPTER FOUR

The pretty glade was just a distant memory.

Carys trudged behind Sten, staring at his broad back. He'd been quiet since he'd rushed to her rescue in the water.

Being held against his hard body, his callused palm caressing her breast...

She almost tripped, her belly fluttering. The man had no clue what he did to her. He'd left her in that small pool with her skin itchy and hot need thrumming through her.

How many times had she touched herself, thinking about him? She bit her lip, feeling a little guilty.

He'd barely looked at her for the last hour. Her shoulders slumped. She'd been naked, and he couldn't get away fast enough.

She focused on walking. They were headed back down into another deep ravine. There had been no other way to cross it. She paused, staring out across the mountains. A wind had picked up and tugged at her hair. The mountain range had a rugged beauty, despite the danger. They reminded her a bit of Sten.

"Carys?"

He was farther down the path, looking back at her.

She hurried to catch up to him.

"Stay alert," he warned. "There are no doubt more alien beasts down here."

She nodded. She was still worried about how they were going to get off this planet. Her stomach turned over. The Gek'Dragar were planning something. It was the only reason why they would've taken her.

They wanted to destabilize the Oronis, and use her to do it. She wasn't sure exactly what they had planned, but she knew it would be nothing good.

She swallowed. She had to save her people.

It was times like this that she wished her parents were still alive. Her heart squeezed. That she had someone to talk to.

It was easy to feel alone sometimes. She could be standing in the middle of a crowded ballroom, with dozens of people desperate to talk to her, and still feel alone.

"Hey." Sten grabbed her arm. Then he held out a water bottle. "Drink."

Only one person in her life made her feel like she wasn't alone. Sten was always there for her.

Because it's his job.

She sipped the water, pushing that thought away. She needed to focus. She needed all her concentration to get across this ravine unscathed. Leaning against the rock wall, she scanned around.

Then she frowned.

Another narrow path, barely discernible, branched off, running up over part of the rocky hill. Probably made by some of the wild animals. She took a step forward and saw a glimmer of something at the top of the rise.

"Carys?"

She handed him back the bottle. "I saw something reflect from up there."

Sten spun, a hand pressed to his hip. Then he straightened. "I see it."

"We should check it out."

He frowned. "It could be Gek'Dragar."

"Or it could be something that might help us. We'll be careful."

"As my queen commands."

They left the main path and started up the hillside. It was steeper than she'd realized and in places, she had to grip the rocks to haul herself up. Smaller rocks skittered under her feet.

Sten was several steps ahead of her and reached the rise first. He stopped.

Breathing heavily, she moved up beside him and gasped. "What the—?"

The top of this part of the mountain was flat. It was covered in small rocks and dirt, but ahead, was a patch of metal. That's what she'd seen.

"This isn't natural," she said.

Sten shook his head. "No. It's too flat, and look at that curve." He pointed.

The edge of the plateau was a perfect semi-circle, projecting out over the side of the mountain.

"Maybe it's a temple, or something?" She made her way toward the metal. Crouching, she used her hand to clear some of the smaller rocks and debris away.

Definitely silver metal. She saw some sort of alien writing etched into the metal. "Sten, what do you think this is?"

"I think this entire area is metal." He looked down and sucked in a breath. "And that's an airlock door."

Carys gasped. "By the knights, this is a ship?"

Crouching beside her, he moved his hand over the metal. He found a flap and lifted it. Under it were three round black buttons. Sten touched them, and a second later, there was a hiss and a *thunk*. He jerked his hand back, just as a circular piece of metal retracted and slid open.

Leaving a hole and a ladder leading downward.

"Sten, a ship!" Excitement winged through her. "It might be operational. It'll definitely have some sort of comms system."

His brow furrowed. "It looks like it's been here a long time, Carys. It probably crash-landed. We have no idea what condition—"

She scrambled onto the ladder. "Only one way to find out." She gripped the rungs.

"Carys," he growled. "Let me go first."

"Too late." She headed down the ladder.

She heard him grumbling as he followed her. *Good.*

Then guilt hit her. He was worried about her safety. It wasn't his fault he'd hurt her feelings.

She had to put that moment in the pool behind her.

Climbing off the ladder, she looked around.

The ship was in a bad state. Panels had fallen from the ceiling and cables dangled everywhere. Chairs had been ripped from the floor and flung around. Dust covered everything.

Sten's boots clunked on the floor, and he looked around too. "I don't recognize the design."

Carys didn't either. Ducking some cables, she headed toward the front of the ship.

"Carys, be careful."

She half expected to find some bodies or skeletons of whoever the ship had belonged to, but thankfully, she didn't see any. She squeezed through a damaged doorway and into the cockpit.

There were four curved seats in front of a long control panel. Old scorch marks told her there had been a fire. She wondered what had happened to the people who'd crashed here. The viewscreen was covered in grime, but through one clear patch, she saw the ravine below.

The ship was perched right on the edge of the cliff, but she figured since it had been here for decades, it was safe enough.

She tried the control panel. "Nothing." Frustration chewed at her.

Sten slid a hand over the built-in screen. "No power." He dropped down and slid under the console. "Let me take a look." He yanked a panel off.

"I didn't know you were any good with ship systems." She perched on the edge of a chair and watched him work.

"I'm not. But you know I grew up on a farm. My

father could fix every bit of equipment he had. He taught me a few things."

Sten rarely talked about himself or his family. All she knew was that his mother had died when he'd been young, and he'd been raised by his father.

"Have you seen your father lately?"

He yanked on some wires, then paused. "He died nine months ago."

Carys gasped. "You never told me! You didn't take any time off."

"There was nothing to be done. I saw to his funeral." His tone was gruff.

"Time off to grieve, Sten."

"I didn't need time."

She looked up at the ceiling. The man drove her crazy sometimes. "Losing someone important to you hurts."

"He'd lived a good, honest life."

She looked back and saw he was watching her.

"Dad was proud of me for becoming a knight. He died content."

Sten was alone now too, like she had been for so long. "Sten—"

He touched some wires together and there was a shower of sparks. Lights flickered to life on the console.

She leaped to her feet. "You did it."

"It's only emergency power." He rose and dusted off his hands.

Carys swiped the control panel. "I can't read this text, but hopefully it's got a standard configuration for the system." She tapped and swiped, trying to find the communications. "Got it." She pressed the screen.

A red warning flashed up.

Her heart sank. "That doesn't look good."

Sten pressed his palm to the screen and stared ahead. "Let me see if I can connect via my implants."

She saw his eyes flicker, then he pulled his hand away.

She read it in his face. "It's not functional."

He shook his head. "The communication array was destroyed. There's no way to transmit a message."

STEN WATCHED CARYS WHIRL, then kick a chair.

"*Ow.*" She hopped a little and made a frustrated sound.

"Hey." He knew he shouldn't touch her, but he wanted to comfort her. He settled his palms over her shoulders. "We'll find a way off this planet."

"How long will that take?" She sagged back against him. "The Gek'Dragar are planning an attack, I can feel it. I need to protect our people."

"Ashtin and the others already know the Gek'Dragar are a threat. They'll be ready." He slid an arm around her and rested his chin on the top of her head. "It's going to be all right."

She pulled in a ragged breath. "I want to believe that." She pressed her hand to his arm. "Is this the moment where you pull away from me like I have the tellarian flu?"

He stiffened. "It isn't right that I'm touching you."

"It feels right to me." She brushed her fingers over his arm. "I like you touching me, Sten."

Gul. He fought back a shudder.

"I liked you touching me earlier." Her voice was quiet. "At the pool."

"That should never have happened." He couldn't risk letting free all the things he felt for her. "I'm your knight-guard. I can't be distracted. I can't…"

She turned and looked up at him. Her eyes looked like melted gold. "We're allowed to feel. I'm not just a queen, you know."

"I know."

Her lips tightened. "I don't think you do. I'm a woman, and being this close to you…" She stroked a hand up his arm. "It makes me want so many things."

Gul. "Carys—"

A sudden explosion rocked the ship. She collided with his chest, and he caught her.

"What was that?" she cried.

Alarms blared from the control console. Sten staggered toward it. He cursed.

"What?" She gripped his arm.

"The emergency power's built up in damaged parts of the engine. It's—"

Another explosion. This one shot the ship forward.

Sten felt it tip. He grabbed Carys and watched as the viewscreen dipped.

Giving them a view down into the ravine below.

She clung to him. "It's going over the edge!"

Instinct took over. Sten stooped and threw Carys over

his shoulder. He charged out of the cockpit, climbing up as the angle of the floor increased.

Metal groaned and objects broke loose, raining down on them.

There was no time to get out of the ship. They needed somewhere strong enough to withstand the fall. Staggering, he moved down a metal corridor, dodging more debris.

There. A doorway. He shouldered it open and flung himself inside.

He rolled so he landed on the floor first, cushioning Carys.

It was a meeting room of some kind, with a long table bolted to the floor. A floor that was almost vertical now.

"Under the table," he yelled.

She crawled under the table, and he followed. He gripped the table and braced his legs, then pulled her into the shelter of his body.

"Hold on."

She burrowed against him, wrapping her arms around his body.

Metal screeched and for a second, the ship hung motionless.

Then it fell.

He held on tight to the table and Carys. He braced for impact.

"Sten—" Her gaze met his.

He hated seeing her afraid. "I've got you. Keep looking at me."

Crash.

CHAPTER FIVE

Her heart was hammering hard in her chest.
They were jolted roughly, and Carys heard objects crash and shatter.

Then the ship came to a violent stop.

She gripped Sten's body hard. She heard him grunt, but his arms never loosened. No, her knightguard sheltered her. As always, keeping her safe.

"We made it," she whispered.

"You're not hurt?" he asked gruffly.

"No." She twisted to look at him and saw blood sliding down the side of his face. "But you are. You're bleeding."

He carefully let her go and swiped at his temple. "It's just a cut. We need to get out of here. The Gek'Dragar will come to investigate."

With a nod, she swiveled and crawled out. She glanced back and saw he was looking at her ass.

Her pulse did a jagged dance. She saw him drop his chin to his chest and drag in some air.

"Sten?"

"Coming." He slid out from under the table and rose. "We need to move quickly."

They clambered through the ship. A huge hole had been torn in the side of it. Sten leaped out and held his hands up for her. She jumped and he caught her by the waist.

"Well, at least it was a shortcut to the bottom of the ravine," she said.

He shot her a look.

She smiled. She guessed he wasn't quite ready to joke about it. "Not that I want to do it again."

"Come on." He set a fast pace, jogging down the ravine. Rocks crunched underfoot. Carys winced, thankful that her implants blocked most of the pain of walking on her bare feet.

He scanned the skies, and she did the same, searching for any Gek'Dragar scout ships or drones.

Suddenly, a stench hit her. She held her hand to her nose. "What's that smell?"

Sten appeared unaffected. "Something rotting." He strode to a pile of rocks and climbed up. She followed behind him.

On the other side, they discovered the rotting carcass of a strange beast with matted, brown fur.

She wrinkled her nose. Its side had been slashed with sharp claws.

"Come on," Sten said. "Let's cross this ravine fast, and find a way up the next mountainside."

She wasn't going to argue. She wanted to be gone

before whatever had killed that beast found them, or the Gek'Dragar appeared.

They moved across the narrow valley.

It was silent. There was no wind, no rocks falling, nothing.

Carys slowed. She saw Sten looking up.

High overhead, clouds were forming, blocking out the sun. It made the shadows down here much darker. Shadows clung to the rocks and dark spaces at the edge of the chasm. The hairs on the back of her neck rose.

They weren't alone.

All of a sudden, something darted in the shadows. She stared hard, trying to see the shape of it. She formed an energy ball on her palm.

Her energy was coming stronger and more easily now. The lingering effects of the drugs were almost gone. She tried to form her armor, but still nothing. She blew out a frustrated breath.

Movement in the shadows again.

Nearby, Sten formed his sword.

"Can you tell what it is?" she asked.

"No."

"It doesn't look too big," she whispered.

The creature rushed out, opening its jaws wide showing off its needle-like teeth. It had red eyes on each side of its snout. It was small, but powerfully built, with wicked spikes along its back.

Carys formed a small energy ball and threw it. It hit the creature and it made a horrible noise, snapping its jaws.

She frowned. As she watched, it snapped at the energy ball.

She threw another one.

"Wait." Sten caught her arm.

The second ball hit the creature. It tossed its head back, gulping the crackling energy down its throat. Its body bulged and grew.

Horror filled her. "It's feeding on the energy."

The now-larger animal tossed its head back and roared. Then its red gaze locked on them, and it charged.

Sten leaped forward and sliced with his sword. He and the animal danced around each other. He slashed again, striking a glancing blow.

The animal suddenly twisted and raced at Carys.

Heart pounding, she ran at it, then dropped down sliding beneath it. She formed energy spikes on her hands, like claws, and jammed them up into the creature's underbelly.

It let out a deafening roar.

Blood splattered, and she rolled to her feet and spun. Sten appeared beside her, and they charged together.

He slashed with his sword and Carys whipped up her energy gauntlets. She and Sten worked together fighting the creature.

Carys distracted it, slicing again with her energy claws across its snout.

It roared, but she kept its attention long enough for Sten to slide in, and ram his sword into the creature's side.

This time, it didn't make a sound. Its body shuddered, then it collapsed on the rocks.

Sten stepped back, lowering his sword. He turned to Carys. "Very fierce, my queen."

She grinned at him. "Thank you, my knightguard." She let her gauntlets dissolve away. "I had a good teacher."

He reached out, wiping his finger across her cheek.

Her breath hitched.

"You have some blood here," he murmured.

Energy from the fight was still pounding through her, and the touch of his fingers added to the sensation. She felt heat wash over her skin.

Sten paused, his gaze locking with hers.

She gripped his wrist, felt the fast beat of his pulse.

That's when they heard shouts.

Sten bit out a curse. Her pulse spiking, Carys spun.

Five Gek'Dragar soldiers sprinted into view, lifting their weapons. Her heart leaped into her throat, but at the same time, resolve firmed inside her.

Finally, she could face the enemy who'd taken her. The ones who were hunting them like they were animals.

Sten lifted his sword.

"There are only five," she said. "We can take them."

Sten's mouth flattened but he nodded. Then his brow creased.

"What?" she said.

"I think..." Suddenly, black bands of armor, made from a nanotech substance, snapped into place over his broad chest.

Carys gasped. She knew the armor was flowing from the implants embedded along his spine. It covered his body, flowing down his arms and legs, before a black visor slid over his face.

She reached deep, connecting with her *oralite* implant. For a second, there was nothing. Panic flared as she watched the Gek'Dragar running toward them.

Then, it felt like a wave crashing through a barrier.

Her armor formed.

As the black armor slid over her body, it felt like she'd regained the use of a limb. Power flared inside her.

Her visor slid closed, combat information running down the screen. Her own sword formed in her hand, glowing bright blue.

"Be careful." Sten's deep voice came through her implant's comm line.

She lifted her sword in front of her. "Being careful isn't what we need right now."

She wanted to fight. She *needed* to fight. Most of all, she wanted revenge.

STEN THRUST HIS SWORD FORWARD.

The Gek'Dragar soldier dodged, but Sten was filled with the savage need to protect his queen.

His next thrust cut through the enemy's heavy armor and leathery skin.

He felt the rush of Carys' energy and knew she'd engaged the other soldiers. The Gek'Dragar sliced at Sten's shoulder, and he hammered a quick punch to the alien's horned face.

The Gek'Dragar made a low, garbled sound.

Sten's next thrust was to his enemy's gut. He kicked the Gek'Dragar back, freeing his sword.

He saw Carys send a giant energy wave into two Gek'Dragar soldiers, knocking them off their feet.

The other two charged at Sten.

He swung and struck one. He whirled, hooked the second alien's leg with his, and yanked him off his feet.

But the first Gek'Dragar was already rushing at him, holding his large, clawed hand up. He felt the kiss of the soldier's blade on his armor.

His armor held, but he felt the power of the blow. Ignoring the pain, he rammed an elbow into the Gek'-Dragar's jaw.

The alien staggered back, then he let out a low roar.

As Sten watched, the soldier's body started to enlarge, muscles rippling.

Sten's gut clenched. The *var*. A battlefield transformation that allowed the Gek'Dragar to get larger, stronger, wilder.

The alien towered over Sten and yanked a blaster off his belt. Sten glared.

Bring it.

The soldier fired and Sten dodged. He crashed into the attacker, driving him backward. Stepping back, Sten swung his sword up. The Gek'Dragar lifted his hand. They were now tipped with long, black claws.

Sword met claw, Sten's blue blade sizzling against the Gek'Dragar's hand.

They whirled, striking again. The Gek'Dragar was stronger and more powerful under the influence of the *var*.

KNIGHTQUEEN

Sten swung his sword, over and over, but the soldier deflected every blow.

"Come on," Sten roared.

But when a heavy weight slammed into his back, he realized the soldier had been distracting him. Waiting for the second Gek'Dragar to attack.

Claws rammed into his side, piercing his armor. It felt like fire. He gritted his teeth, pain rocketed through him.

He rammed an elbow back, catching the second attacker in the face. He whirled and jumped, using his enhancements to jump above his opponents' heads.

A powerful slash decapitated the first soldier.

Sten landed, blood dripping off his sword. He spun and caught a glimpse of Carys fighting with another Gek'Dragar. Her sword whirled gracefully.

"You will not touch my queen," he growled at the soldier in front of him.

The Gek'Dragar sneered. "We will take her, torture her, and kill her. We will kill *all* Oronis scum."

Sten roared and charged. His blade hit a weak spot on the Gek'Dragar's armor, and his fury pushed him. He rammed the blade right through the Gek'Dragar. He saw the light wink out of the alien's eyes, then his body collapsed.

Sten sensed another one coming in for the attack. He swiveled, but knew he wouldn't be fast enough.

The Gek'Dragar swung a huge mace. It hit the side of Sten's head, and the world wavered, his ears ringing.

He stumbled back.

He raised his sword and glanced at Carys.

She looked up. "Sten!"

He had to protect her. He couldn't fail her.

The Gek'Dragar lifted his mace above his head. "I will kill you, then I will kill her."

Sten lunged forward. The Gek'Dragar brought his mace down on Sten's sword, pinning it. But he missed the blue energy knife forming in a flash in Sten's left hand.

Sten sliced it through a joint in the alien's armor, right through his thigh.

It hit something vital, blood gushing.

The Gek'Dragar made a horrible sound. He dropped his mace, then fumbled.

Too late, Sten realized the alien had pulled his own knife. He rammed it into Sten's side, right where the other Gek'Dragar had pierced his armor.

Sten grunted, and felt hot liquid drench his hip.

The Gek'Dragar stared at him, hatred in his neon-green eyes. Sten could feel the alien's need to fight and kill.

Filled with protective fury, Sten headbutted the Gek'Dragar. Then he stabbed his knife into the enemy's neck, deep. He pulsed energy through the weapon.

Dead, the Gek'Dragar fell backward.

Then Sten dropped to his knees. The pain was too much, blood soaking down his side.

"Sten!"

Everything wavered. Carys' face came into view, her helmet retracting.

"You're hurt." She cupped his cheek.

"It'll heal." But it hurt badly. It took everything he had to stay conscious. "The Gek'Dragar?"

"They're all dead." Worry creased her face. "I hate

seeing you hurt."

He liked that. That she worried about him. "We can't stay here. More Gek'Dragar will come."

"I know. Catch your breath, then we'll go."

"I'm fine."

She rolled her eyes. "You're so stubborn. The blood running down your side says otherwise."

She wrapped an arm around him and then helped him up. He knew her armor would give her extra strength to lift him. Once he was on his feet, nausea spun through him.

"You're stubborn too," he said. "You hide it under polite smiles and cool looks, but you're as stubborn as *wesium* steel."

"And you're as unmoving as a rock." She looked sideways. "There's one thing we need to do before we go."

The pain was making it hard to concentrate. He followed her gaze and that's when he saw one Gek'-Dragar soldier tied up. He was breathing heavily and injured.

"You kept one alive."

She nodded. "I have questions."

She helped Sten lean against the cliff face, then she turned to the enemy.

"What are the Gek'Dragar's plans for Oron?"

The enemy soldier just glared.

Carys crouched. "I know you're in pain, and I don't want to make it worse, but I can."

He sneered. "You and your kind are weak."

She pressed her palm to his slashed arm, and blue light glowed. He cried out. "Don't think because I am a just and empathetic leader that I won't do the difficult things required to protect my people. Your species has attacked mine so many times, and attacked and subjugated others. You just tried to kill me and my guard."

Another flare of blue. The Gek'Dragar leaned forward and dry heaved.

"Why did you abduct me?" Her voice was sharper than a blade.

The alien bared his teeth. "To send your people into a panic. To prepare for what is to come, and make it easier for us to destroy the Oronis."

"How?"

Now, he smiled, his expression hideous. "Consumed in the most beautiful way. Our weapon will destroy you all."

Sten frowned. *Weapon?* "What weapon?"

"The end of Oron is coming." The Gek'Dragar raised his voice. "Soon, my people will launch their attack. You will die, Knightqueen, like all your people. We will make you watch the destruction. The Gek'Dragar will prevail. We are the strongest of all—"

Sten had had enough. He formed his sword, then stabbed the Gek'Dragar through the neck.

The Gek'Dragar choked, then slumped forward.

Carys arched a brow at Sten.

"I couldn't take anymore," he grumbled.

"Come on." She leaned into him. "We need to go."

They hobbled across the ravine and started up the path on the other side.

"It'll be dark again soon. We need shelter." But he was in no condition to find shelter for them. Even just walking was an exercise in agony. He didn't tell her, but he was bleeding internally.

They hobbled up the path. A wind blew in, making Carys' hair dance. They glanced across the mountains, and he exhaled forcefully.

Clouds were blowing in. Fast.

A storm.

Lightning speared through the clouds, followed by a crack of thunder. The wind picked up, blowing hard against them.

"Keep moving," she said grimly.

"If the wind gets worse, it'll knock us off this path."

"Positive thinking, Thorsten."

The wind got stronger. Soon they were walking half bent over, fighting for every step. Little rocks started pelting them. One hit Carys' cheek, drawing blood.

With a gasp, she pressed a hand to her face. Jaw tight, Sten shouldered in front of her, shielding her with his body.

"Sten, you're hurt," she protested.

"Doesn't change anything." It was his duty to keep her safe.

They moved a little farther, and he realized it was getting harder and harder to see. Despair engulfed him. He needed to find somewhere safe for Carys.

But they were stuck on a narrow cliff path with a deadly drop right beside them.

"Look," she said suddenly.

He stared into the swirling dust and frowned. A circular shape lay ahead.

A mine entrance.

CHAPTER SIX

The storm was getting worse.

As rocks peppered her, Carys winced. They reached the metal door to the mine, and she saw the control panel on the side, built into the rock. She rapped her hand against the buttons but nothing was working.

"There's no power."

Sten moved up beside her, moving slowly. It wasn't like him. Her belly curdled. She knew he was hurt badly.

But the stubborn man would never admit it.

She blew out a breath, then she gritted her teeth and sent a surge of energy into the panel. She watched the blue light crackle over the controls, and a second later, the door groaned open.

"Sten, quickly."

He almost stumbled, and she slid an arm around him. He was heavy, all thick muscle. She gritted her teeth and helped him stay upright.

They staggered inside, and she quickly turned and touched the interior controls. She slammed her palm against the panel and the door closed, cutting off the storm.

It plunged them into pitch darkness.

Carys held out her palm and ignited a small energy ball. In the blue light, she watched Sten lean against the wall. His face was ashen.

Tamping down her worry, she looked around. She spotted some dusty gear stacked by the door and waded through it. She found a small lantern.

She turned the dials, praying it still had power, and a second later, it flared to life. A warm, golden light emitted from it.

She set it down. "You're hurt."

"I'll heal."

"Sten."

He coughed, and she saw blood on his lips. Her pulse spiked. *No, no, no.* Then he collapsed to the ground.

"Sten!" She cupped his jaw. "Retract your armor."

He groaned, but a second later, his armor withdrew.

She saw that his shirt was soaked with blood. She sucked in a breath. It was bad. Really bad.

"You should've told me."

The annoying man just grunted.

She ripped his shirt open. Part of her mind registered the slabs of muscle on his chest covered in a sprinkling of brown hair. His abs were heavy, defined ridges. But her focus lay on the jagged cut on his side. It was still oozing blood.

Her throat tightened. She couldn't lose him.

She'd lost her family, and after that, Sten had become her rock.

The one constant in her life.

He'd looked after her, and he was the one person who didn't see the queen all the time. He didn't expect her to have all the answers.

"You should've told me." Worry sharpened her tone. She retracted her own armor, then ripped fabric off the bottom of her dress. She pressed it against his cut, putting a lot of pressure on it.

He winced. "Nothing...you could do."

"You're in pain." She cupped his cheek.

His green gaze met hers, something deep inside them that she couldn't read. "It'll pass. And any pain is worth it to keep you safe."

Carys bit her lip. "I can't lose you, Sten."

He raised his hand and covered hers. "Do my best not to go anywhere." The corner of his lips lifted. "And I always obey my queen."

Worry and love mixed inside her. "I'm going to search for a medical kit, or bandages. Something to help you."

"No." He shifted on the ground. "You'll be unprotected."

"I'm Knightqueen Carys of Oron. I'll protect myself. You know that. And I won't go far."

She hated leaving him, but she turned and made herself walk down the tunnel. She ignited energy on her palm, again using it to guide her way. She hadn't gone far when art and engravings began to emerge on the wall.

She gasped. The images were stunning. The depicted beings were tall and red-skinned. The scenes showed them living in the mountains, in the cliffside villages.

Groups crossing a maze of bridges crisscrossing the ravines. Workers in a mine. She saw that they were mining a bronze powder. She frowned. It looked like they were using another substance—a brilliant, bright-blue liquid—that was part of the mining process.

Dragging her gaze off the artwork, she spotted a doorway covered in cobwebs. She shoved the webs aside.

The room looked like an office and dining area. Several long tables were covered in a thick layer of dust.

She quickly checked the shelves. There had to be some sort of medical kit.

She spotted a black box covered in the markings of an alien language. She pulled it open. Her heart dropped. All that was left was disintegrated powder in the bottom. She opened the next box.

Her pulse leaped. It wasn't exactly like an Oronis medical kit, but there were bandages and other gear. Turning, she hefted the box, and hurried back down the tunnel.

When Sten came into view, he was so still, his eyes closed. Her heart squeezed.

"Sten?"

Green eyes opened. "You okay?"

"Yes." She knelt beside him.

She quickly set to work, tearing open packages.

"I want to sit up," he said.

"No."

His face turned stony. "I don't want—"

She stroked a hand over his short hair. "That's an order, knightguard."

He blew out a breath, and she swiped a medical wipe

over his wound. He hissed. She cleaned his wound, and then the blood off his skin. Then she pressed a thick bandage over his side.

She wished there was more she could do.

"You need time to heal. At least our implants seem to be fully functioning now." She noted her feet had healed, and the faded bruises from the beatings the Gek'Dragar had given him were gone.

A muscle ticked in his jaw.

Carys narrowed her gaze. "Sten? I know you too well. What aren't you telling me?"

He was silent for a moment. "I'm bleeding internally."

Panic lodged in her throat. "No."

"Carys—"

"*No.*" She pressed her hands to his chest. She liked touching his bare skin, loved that he was so warm. Alive. "I *can't* lose you. I won't lose you. That's an order." Her voice trembled.

He gave her a faint smile. "I always follow orders."

She moved her hands down to the bandage. She'd never used her energy to heal. Knighthealers were the ones whose energy was more attuned to healing. She licked her lips. Her mother had been a knighthealer.

There were rumors that the royal blood could access incredible power, but she'd never seen that happen. She was sure it was just a myth.

"Let me see." She pressed a hand over his wound, and the other on one of his thighs for balance.

He stiffened.

"Am I hurting you?"

"No."

Did he really hate her touching him that much? He'd been aroused when he'd touched her in that pool, but her experience was limited, so she had no idea.

Focus, Carys.

"What are you doing?" he asked.

"Seeing if I can heal you." She closed her eyes.

"I've never seen you heal before."

"I've never tried." She focused on Sten's warmth. On her feelings. She couldn't lose him.

She loved how protective he was. How he could be so dogged about her protection, even a little grumpy. He was loyal and true.

She dug deeper and felt something flare inside her. There was a tiny flicker of unfamiliar power.

She focused on it, and the spark grew. Energy spilled out of her.

Sten grunted.

The sensation petered out quickly, and she sat back with a frustrated breath. "I'm sorry."

"I...think it worked. A little." He pushed himself into a sitting position and leaned against the wall. "My wound feels better, and I can feel that my implant is healing me now."

Elation filled her. "Thank the knights."

He cupped her jaw. "You did it. Some days, I think you can do anything."

The praise made her cheeks warm. "Hardly." The feel of his palm made her skin tingle.

She wished he'd touch other parts of her.

"Carys, we can't stay here." He pulled his hand away.

She felt the loss.

"The Gek'Dragar will track us," he continued.

"Not in the storm. We'll wait until you're healed." She sat beside him and rested her head on his shoulder.

He went stiff again, but then he slowly relaxed.

"Sten?"

"My queen?"

"Will you sing to me? Please?"

It had been years since he'd sung for her. He'd done it when she was younger, after the death of her parents.

She looked up, noting the dull color in his cheeks. Her stoic knightguard didn't like anyone knowing that he had a good singing voice.

There was a long pause, then he started to sing.

She smiled and listened to the deep, beautiful baritone. He sang a song about a beautiful princess. A courageous princess.

Carys breathed in. They were safe for now, and Sten was healing. Sten was with her.

Her heart yearned for more from him, more than he could give. But now, as always, she'd take what she could get.

STEN GRITTED his teeth and walked. One foot in front of the other. That was all he could focus on.

If Carys saw that he was in pain, she'd make him rest again. His wounds were healing, but they hurt.

Carys was just two steps ahead of him, holding the lantern aloft to illuminate the darkness.

"Sten, look at these." She moved over to the wall of the tunnel.

He saw engraved artwork, painted in beautiful colors.

"I noticed it earlier, but I was in a rush." She ran a hand over one of the tall, red figures. "I think these people were the local inhabitants of this planet."

In the images, Sten noted bustling, cliff villages, lots of bridges crossing the ravines, and the red-skinned people mining a bronze substance. He stepped closer.

"Senum," he said.

Carys cocked her head. "Really?"

The mineral was prized, and had a lot of applications. He traced the images with his fingers. "It's highly valuable. Especially to Gek'Dragar." He saw the local people using a blue liquid to mine. "Looks like the locals mined the senum with this blue fluid. It eats away at the rock."

They kept walking and the art changed. It was less detailed, sloppier. Like the best artists had gone, or they were running out of time.

Carys gasped. "Sten."

The next image showed Gek'Dragar.

They overtook the planet. In some images, there were large vats of the blue fluid.

"No," Carys whispered.

The scenes changed to show mountains caved in and villages destroyed. The blue fluid eating them away.

Then a final image, showing animals drinking the liquid, and their bodies changing and morphing.

"I guess we know why there are so many terrible beasts," he said grimly. "The Gek'Dragar used the locals' own mining method against them."

"And drove them out." Sadness colored her voice.

She always felt so deeply. Some called her cool, but she was never that. Especially behind closed doors. He'd seen her ranting and crying plenty of times.

Right now, he watched her hand ball into a fist, a fierce look on her face.

"The Gek'Dragar *have* to be stopped. The Oronis drove them back once, but now, they want to fight, kill, take, and cause chaos and destruction like this." She waved at the wall.

"They believe fighting makes them stronger."

She whirled. "It's taking care of your people—your young and old, your weak and sick—that makes you strong. The Oronis are about duty, service. That is strength, not the ability to wield a weapon."

"I know."

She shot him a rueful smile. "I'm preaching to someone who lives and breathes the Oronis creed." She gripped his forearm. "You are the most loyal, noble man I've ever met."

He felt the heat of her touch. He still was unsteady on his feet, and it made it hard to fight the pull she had over him.

She is your queen. Don't forget that.

He dragged in a deep breath and made himself look back at the walls. "Our ancestors fought the brutal wars of Gammis III to defeat the Gek'Dragar. Many knights died."

Carys straightened. "They died heroes. They believed in their creed, believed in protecting their people."

Sten nodded. "Every Oronis knight will stand behind their queen without question. I'll be the first."

Soon, the art stopped, and sadness deepened on Carys' face. He wanted to hold her, soothe her.

His hand flexed.

"I'm guessing the sun must be setting by now," she said.

He nodded. Hopefully the Gek'Dragar wouldn't prowl at night with so many beasts out.

"Let's find somewhere we can bed down for the night," he said.

They moved on, pushing through cobwebs.

He heard a chittering noise and the flutter of wings. He paused.

"Carys." He pulled her back against him.

Small bat-like creatures came out of the darkness. They were tiny, with fluffy bodies, and cute wings. They flitted around them, catching at Carys' hair. He tried to wave them away until she laughed.

"They mean no harm."

His jaw was tight. He wasn't as quick to trust as she was.

The creatures disappeared back into the darkness. A moment later, the tunnel opened up.

"Oh, my stars," Carys murmured.

It was a huge, circular cavern. The ceiling disappeared high above, and, in the distance, he saw faint light. Probably an opening to the sky. Then he looked down.

"Be careful," he warned.

She moved the lantern, highlighting that they weren't far from the edge of a massive hole.

The light didn't go far, and Sten got the sense of a gigantic, endless chasm.

As she lifted the lantern, he spotted something above them. It was the shadow of a rail line crossing above the hole, leading to the other side. No doubt it would be rusted from disuse.

"This way." He walked along the edge of the chasm. "Don't get too close. The edge looks unstable."

When he glanced at her, he caught her rolling her eyes.

"Your safety is my job," he reminded her.

"I know." Her smile slipped away. "And you do your job well, Sten." She looked away from him.

He'd protect her, no matter what it took. No matter if he had to give his life. "If I'd done it right, you wouldn't be here. The Gek'Dragar would never have gotten their hands on you."

She whirled on him. "That's not your fault."

"I'm the head of your knightguard."

She stepped in front of him, and poked him in the chest. "Even you can't predict a secret Gek'Dragar attack that you know nothing about." She shook her head. "I don't want your misplaced guilt, Sten. Come on. We need to find somewhere to sleep. I don't fancy resting on hard rocks."

"You can sleep on me."

Her head jerked up.

Was she blushing? He heaved in a deep breath. He shouldn't have said that. The thought of holding her again...

By the coward's bones, his cock was already twitching in his trousers. How could he keep his control?

She cleared her throat. "We need to find a way across the chasm. That's the direction we need to go."

"That's a problem for tomorrow."

As they walked on, he spotted a glow of blue ahead. He took another step, and something crunched under his boot. Some sort of glass.

Then he saw the puddle of blue liquid resting on a curved shard of glass. He crouched. He grabbed a nearby rock, and touched the puddle.

He watched as it ate into the rock like acid. He quickly dropped the dissolving rock.

"Don't touch it," he warned.

"It's the mining fluid."

"Yes." He scanned it with his implant. "It's a nano-fluid design specifically to consume the minerals in the rock. It will also eat into metal, but at a slower rate. Flesh won't fair well, so keep clear."

She crouched beside him. "It's so pretty for something so dangerous."

They moved on, and soon a stack of mining gear appeared out of the darkness. Sten blew dust off one of the crates and pried open the lid. It contained tools and mining equipment. He opened the next crate. This one was filled with sacks. He opened a sack and pulled out some fabric. It was a uniform made for very tall bodies.

"We can use these sacks to make a bed," he said.

Carys helped him pull some out. They stacked them into a makeshift bed by the wall, far away from the edge of the chasm.

She dropped down on the sacks with a sigh. "How are your injuries?"

"Feeling much better. Whatever you did, it helped heal me." He sat beside her.

"I'm glad." She sighed. "We have no idea how much farther we need to travel."

"We *will* get off this planet," he said. "I vow it."

She pressed a hand over his. "I know, Sten. I'm just tired, and my heart is sore at all this destruction." She looked around. "I won't let our enemies do this to Oron."

She could protect Oron, while he protected her. He'd make sure the Gek'Dragar didn't hurt her again.

"Our first step is getting home. You are the heart of the Oronis."

She let out another sigh. "Sometimes I'm just a woman."

Sten flexed his fingers. He wanted to touch her, but he made himself stand. "Get some sleep. I'll do a security check."

She lay down on the sacks. "Good night, Sten."

It didn't matter that her dress was ripped and dirty, or her feet were bare. She looked beautiful.

He turned and made himself walk away into the darkness.

CHAPTER SEVEN

She was so comfortable.

Carys opened her eyes. It was still pitch black. She felt cool air on her back and blazing heat on her front.

Then she realized where she was. In the mine.

Wrapped up in Sten's arms.

Her belly fluttered. She turned her face into his neck and his arms tightened around her. He held her flush against his hard body. She shuddered out a breath, and desire filled her—hot and sharp. In his sleep, his hand slid down and cupped her ass.

Oh. It made her yearn for more. For touches, caresses. For sex. She'd shared a few uninspired kisses here and there, but that was it.

Sex was too complicated when you were a queen, and your entire planet was watching. At least, that was her excuse.

She breathed Sten in. The truth was, there was only

one man she imagined peeling her clothes off, touching her, putting his hands on her skin.

The one man who didn't want her.

For now, she'd steal this moment. She rubbed her face against his chest. So warm. Safe. She drifted back to sleep.

CARYS OPENED HER EYES, shaking off sleep. She was still tired.

Wait, she wasn't in her bedroom in the palace.

She blinked at the mine roof that soared overhead. The small lantern was on low, giving off a golden glow. The walls were a dark rock, black and forbidding. She could tell it was still nighttime.

She stretched her sore muscles. The lumpy sacks didn't make the most comfortable bed.

The spot beside her was empty. *Where was Sten?* She sat up, touching the depression where he'd been lying. Her knightguard was missing, but she knew he wouldn't be far away.

She already missed touching him. Missed the sense of safety she only felt in his arms. She pushed her hair back and finger combed it. A faint noise caught her ear, and she straightened.

A low groan.

Sten?

Was it his injuries? She rose, and, as quietly as she could, she moved toward the sound. She rounded a corner and saw Sten. He was turned away from her, shirtless.

Her gaze ran greedily over the slabs of muscle in his back. He was built for strength and power.

Then his head dropped forward, and he groaned again.

She took another step, and everything inside her clenched tight.

His pants were undone, his cock free.

Oh.

He was stroking himself roughly.

She flushed and damp heat built between her thighs. He was touching himself. Stroking his cock. She knew she should walk away, but she couldn't.

She was frozen.

But her body was far too hot to be frozen.

She hungrily drank him in and licked her lips. His cock was long, thick, and ruddy. He groaned, his hand moving faster.

She pressed her thighs together and her nipples beaded. His muscles were so tense, strained, and she saw a grimace cross his face.

He muttered a curse, his hips thrusting forward. "Yes. *Carys.*"

She saw fluid hit the ground as he jerked his cock. Her mind went blank.

He'd said her name.

He finished coming with a low groan, and she quickly turned. She moved silently back to their bed. With every step, her thighs rubbed together, and she felt close to coming, herself.

She dropped back onto the sacks, and pressed her hands to her flushed cheeks.

He'd said her name as he'd found his release.

He'd touched himself while thinking of her.

Sten wanted her.

Emotions crashed through her.

Thorsten Carahan, the man she loved, wanted her.

Nerves coiled in her belly. He was a man. He was older, more experienced. She felt a slash of jealousy. She'd never seen him with a woman, but she hated anyone he might have touched.

She heard him returning and quickly lay back down, pretending to be asleep.

He flicked off the lantern, plunging them into darkness. Then he dropped onto the sacks.

"Sten?" she murmured.

"Sorry for waking you." He lay down. "We've only been asleep a few hours. Go back to sleep."

"I'm cold."

Instantly, he moved closer.

As she pressed into him, she bit her lip.

They were in a terrible situation. They had no idea what planet they were on, and they were being hunted by the Gek'Dragar.

Sten had vowed to get her home, but she was realistic enough to know that they might not make it.

Did she have the courage to ask for what she wanted from him?

For what she'd only dreamed about?

There was no way she wanted to risk dying without ever having been with him.

"You're so tense." He stroked her hair. "Sleep. You're safe."

She drew in a steadying breath. "I don't want to sleep."

He was quiet for a second. "What do you want?"

She paused and gathered her courage. *Remember, you're a grown woman. You're the knightqueen.*

"I want you to kiss me."

STEN WENT RIGID.

Was he dreaming? He was pretty sure he was awake.

Had Carys just asked him to kiss her?

Emotions churned inside him, burning away at the bit of control he thought he'd found when he'd taken his cock in his own hand.

Sleeping beside her for the last few hours—touching her, holding her. It had been torture. Every one of her breaths had puffed across his chest. Every time she moved, her breasts rubbed against him. He now knew exactly what her full breasts looked like, felt like in his palm.

His cock had been hard as a rock for hours. He'd been forced to find some release before he did something he regretted.

He cleared his throat. "Carys—"

"Please, Sten." She curled into him, her hand on his chest. Over the heavy thud of his heart.

"It's not right."

"It feels right." She leaned closer, and her breasts pressed to his chest.

He closed his eyes. She was so soft.

"We're in danger," she said. "We might die here."

He growled. "We are *not* going to die here."

"I want you to kiss me."

"Because I'm the only man around?" The thought sliced at him. He was older, scarred, a big brute compared to her. He wasn't right for her.

"No." There was a rustle as she sat up. A hand touched his cheek. "I've wanted you to kiss me for a very long time."

That couldn't be true. This beautiful, perfect woman wanted him?

He couldn't get that to make sense.

Both her hands pressed to his chest. She leaned in. "Sten..."

"I'm too old. I'm your guard."

"You're only twelve years older than me, Sten. Hardly ancient. And you're a dedicated knightguard. A good man. A strong, attractive man."

"Carys—"

"I want you to kiss me. And...I know you want me, too." Her words were a hot whisper.

His brow creased. "What?"

"I saw you. Just before. Touching yourself."

Heat flushed through him. Embarrassment mixed with desire. He imagined her watching him, and his cock had no problem thickening again.

He surged up, his chest heaving.

She sat as well, shifting closer. "I liked it."

"Stars... Carys...," He felt like his control was slipping through his hands like sand.

Her body moved, brushing against his back. "*Please, Sten.*"

He groaned and tugged her onto his lap. She gasped.

He cupped her elegant face and touched his lips to hers. They brushed. "It's *not* right."

"What if I ordered you to?" She sounded breathless.

His hands clenched on her. "I would never refuse your command."

"Then I order you to kiss me."

He deserved to be skewered with a sword for what he was about to do.

He closed his mouth over hers.

An inferno ignited in his chest, and he groaned against her lips. Her hands clenched on him, and she kissed him back eagerly.

He explored her mouth, loving the small sounds she made. He stroked his tongue against hers. She tasted like the purest Avernian honey.

"Harder," she panted against his lips. "More. Show me more."

He deepened the kiss. *Mine. Take more.*

She arched into him. So hot, so eager. She bit his lip, rubbing against him. She fumbled for one of his hands and brought it to her breast.

He groaned. "You're so perfect."

"Teach me. No one's ever touched me like this."

He'd been her knightguard for over a decade. He suspected that she'd never been with a man. He never truly wanted to know if someone had put their hands on her.

"You're untouched." He nipped her lips.

"Yes, because there was only one man who I wanted to touch me."

Stars, his cock was hard. He pushed the neckline of her dress down and her breasts popped free. She arched her back, offering herself to him.

He pinched one nipple between his fingers. "Beautiful."

She moaned.

He took her mouth again, kissing her deeply as he kept teasing her nipples. She writhed, his hard cock wedged against her ass.

"I want everything, Sten," she whispered against his lips. "I want you to show me everything." She ground down on his cock.

He wanted inside her. The idea of teaching her all the things that would give her pleasure made his gut knot. He wanted to gorge himself on this woman.

His queen.

The thought intruded—cold and sharp.

His queen.

He pulled back.

She was panting. One hand twisted in his hair. "Sten?"

She was his queen. The woman he'd vowed to protect for his entire life.

And he was imagining rutting on her like an animal.

He dumped her on their makeshift bed and sat on the edge of the sacks, staring into the darkness.

"Sten? Did I do something wrong?"

"No." His fists curled. But he had.

She shifted. "What, then? Why did you stop?"

"I told you this isn't right. I can't do this."

He sensed her wrap her arms around herself. "I enjoyed it. Didn't you?"

Enjoyed it? He'd wanted to kiss her forever.

Wanted to hold onto her forever.

She isn't yours.

In his head, he pictured her sitting on the throne. Some handsome prince at her side. A man who'd be a leader, a king for the Oronis. That wasn't him.

He tasted bile in his throat.

"No," he bit out.

"*Oh.*" There was hurt in her voice. "But you were...hard."

"Doesn't take much to make a man hard."

She made a small sound. "I see."

"It's not my place to kiss you, my queen," he said stiffly.

She was silent now. "You only kissed me because I ordered you to?"

He closed his eyes and lied. "Yes."

Another pause. "I'm sorry."

This time her voice was near soundless, and held no expression.

He couldn't stand it. He shot to his feet. "Go back to sleep, Carys. I'll keep watch. Once I know it's daylight, we'll find a way out of this mine."

"Yes, all right. Thank you." Her tone was stiff.

He wanted to turn and yank her into his arms, show her just how much he wanted her.

How hard his cock was for her.

Show her just how he wanted to worship her.

She's not yours. She's too good for you.

He made himself walk away.

CHAPTER EIGHT

Carys stared out over the yawning abyss.
It reflected how she felt inside.
Empty.

No, that wasn't true. Deep down, she wasn't empty. Far within lay a hard ball of hurt.

Sten stepped up beside her, scowling as he scanned the mine.

"We could cross the chasm using the mine railway line." She tried to keep her tone brisk and businesslike.

"It looks too dangerous. We can't risk it failing. I suggest we go back out the way we came in."

She nodded. "As you wish."

She knew her tone was cool and stilted, but right now, she couldn't make herself care. She watched his shoulders stiffen.

He shot her a frustrated glance, but she turned away. She couldn't deal with his feelings on top of her own right now.

"Carys—"

She started walking. "We should get moving, Thorsten." Something twisted in her chest. He might have hurt her, but she still loved the man. "How's your injury?"

"It's almost healed thanks to whatever you did to it."

"Good."

He'd restocked his pack with what he'd found in the mining gear, and swung it over his shoulder. They walked in silence back toward the entrance. The art on the wall looked duller today.

When they neared the mine entrance, a loud clang echoed through the tunnel.

They froze, and Sten grabbed her bicep.

There was another clang.

"Someone's trying to break through the door," he said.

The Gek'Dragar.

Of course, they did everything with brute force. She glared at the doorway, the need to fight them churning inside her.

Sten swiveled and pulled her back down the tunnel. "We have to find another way out."

Her heart rate picked up. Right now, they were trapped between the enemy and a really deep hole.

"Armor on." As he said the words, his armor formed, snapping into place on his body.

With a simple thought, Carys activated her own armor. It felt so good to have full control of her implants again. She watched the black flow down over her arms and legs.

KNIGHTQUEEN

Back at the chasm, Sten shoved his hands on his hips.

"We have to risk the mine rail," she said.

A muscle ticked in his jaw.

"Sten, we're out of options."

He gave her a brisk nod.

They hurried toward the platform where several mine carts sat, hanging from the mine rail. As they neared, she saw more of the metal track. It was rusty in places, and covered in dust. Her stomach clenched.

"Uh, it's not in great condition."

"No." His tone was unhappy. "But the Gek'Dragar are definitely not safe. Like you said, we're out of options. I haven't found any other way out of here. I looked while you were sleeping."

While she'd been lying in that bed alone and he'd been avoiding her. She steeled herself and nodded.

Sten stepped into the first cart. It hung off the rail above and there were two seats in front of a control console. A huge empty cart dangled underneath for carrying the mining ore.

She stepped inside, then heard shouts echo through the mine.

The Gek'Dragar were inside.

Sten dropped onto one seat. "Come on."

The cart wobbled a little as she slipped onto the seat beside him. The chasm yawned ahead of them.

Stars, if the rail broke...

It was going to be a long drop.

Focus, Carys. Stay positive.

Sten touched the controls and the panel lit up.

"There's power." He pressed some buttons and the cart lurched forward. Carys gripped onto the console.

Then they started moving.

She decided not to look down. She focused her gaze straight ahead. They were halfway across the huge chasm when the shouts got louder. She looked back over her shoulder.

She saw several Gek'Dragar soldiers standing at the edge of the hole, pointing at them.

And lifting their weapons.

"Sten, down!" She yanked on his arm.

They both ducked as laser fire lit up the space around them. Sten shifted, covering her body with his. The cart rocked and came to a stop.

Her chest squeezed. She *wasn't* going back to their prison.

Sten reached up toward the controls, but more laser fire hit.

"I could—" She didn't finish. There was a low rumble of sound and vibration. She frowned. "What is that?"

"I'm not sure." His fingers tightened on her arms. "It's coming from...below us."

She saw the Gek'Dragar had stopped firing, and were looking around in apparent confusion. The sound got louder.

"Sten."

His hand engulfed hers and squeezed.

Suddenly, a cloud of large, flying creatures streamed up out of the mine. They filled the cavern.

Carys cried out. Wings flapped in her face, and tiny fangs ripped at her hair.

Sten smacked them off her, and covered her with his body again.

"*Gul*," he gritted out.

The creatures kept streaming up, like a giant, black cloud. She heard the Gek'Dragar soldiers' guttural shouts.

Sten swore.

Peering around Sten's brawny arm, she saw three creatures clinging to a Gek'Dragar. They lifted the soldier off his feet, and the soldier kicked and screamed.

The creatures flew out over the chasm...then dropped the soldier. The Gek'Dragar screamed as he fell. Meanwhile, other creatures were tearing at the remaining soldiers.

"We need to get out of here." Sten shifted back to the controls.

A second later, the mining cart started moving again.

A flying creature landed on the front of the cart and screeched.

Oh, stars. She realized it was an adult version of the cute little bats they'd seen earlier. But as adults, they were no longer fluffy or friendly. This one had a sharp beak and leathery wings.

She summoned an energy ball and threw it at the creature. It knocked it off the cart, its screech echoing down into the hole.

The cart picked up speed, clanging on the rail. They turned a corner and spiraled downward.

Her stomach dropped as they went faster and faster.

Suddenly, a rock wall loomed ahead.

"Sten!"

He cursed and thumped at the controls. "The cart won't slow down."

Her throat closed. They were careening right toward the rock wall.

Sten yanked her down. She clung to him.

She didn't want to die.

Just as they neared the wall, a hole suddenly opened up in the center of it.

There was a door hidden in the rock! They'd clearly triggered some sort of opening mechanism.

They sailed through the arched gap.

STEN KEPT a tight hold on Carys as their mining cart zoomed into another cavern. There was enough light filtering in from somewhere for him to see thick, bronze veins of ore glowing in the walls.

Senum.

He arched his neck to look down. Below them lay another deep, yawning darkness.

Suddenly, the cart dipped downward like a wild ride. Carys screamed, and he tightened his hold. She clung to his shirt, fingers digging into his skin.

Thankfully, the cart evened out, and he blew out a breath. He had no idea where they were going, but at least they'd slowed to a more sedate pace.

Shakily, Carys pulled away from him. "Well, that was wild."

She wouldn't meet his gaze. Hadn't since they'd woken up this morning.

His gut felt like it was filled with rocks.

He'd lied to her, and in the process, he'd hurt her. *It's for the best.* His hands flexed. It was what he had to keep telling himself.

I am Knightguard Thorsten Carahan. It is my duty to protect my queen. I am her sword, her shield, and her devoted servant.

He'd spent years trying to lock down his feelings for her.

Now she wouldn't even look at him.

Get her out of this safely. That's all he could focus on right now.

The cart picked up speed again, and his gut lurched. "Stay down. We need—"

The low, rumbling noise grew again. More flying creatures were coming.

He cursed.

They streamed upward from the blackness like a nightmare. Sten formed an energy ball and threw it. They scattered, their wild screeches hurting his ears. The ball hit the rock wall, sending rocks tumbling down into the chasm. He threw another energy ball. This one clipped some of creatures, and he saw them slam into the rail above. The entire structure shuddered.

"Maybe don't knock the already unstable mine rail down," Carys said with a gasp. "At least not while we're hanging from it."

He grunted.

Thankfully, the cloud of flying creatures arrowed downward and disappeared.

"I see light ahead." She leaned forward. "What is that?"

A bluish glow lay in the distance, growing brighter.

Suddenly, the cart jolted to a hard stop.

Sten staggered, but managed to catch himself.

Carys wasn't as lucky.

In horror, he watched her lose her balance, waving her arms. Then she tipped over the edge of the cart with a sharp cry.

"Carys!" He lunged forward.

He gripped the control console with one hand and thrust his other arm over the edge. He caught her hand and held on tight.

She hung below him. Thankfully she was a knight, so she didn't kick or scream in panic.

"Sten..." Her voice was strained.

"I've got you."

She looked down, then quickly jerked her gaze back to his. "Please, don't let go."

"I'll never let you go."

Stunning gold eyes stayed locked on his. "I know. I trust you more than I trust anyone."

He felt a wrench in his chest, then hauled her up and back into the cart.

Crouched in the bottom, she blew out a breath and pressed a hand to her chest. "Let's *not* do that again."

Then he yanked her to him.

She was stiff at first, but then she relaxed. "I'm okay."

Sten needed a second. He closed his eyes and held her tight. In his head, he kept seeing her fall over the edge.

There was no universe he could envisage without Carys in it.

Life wasn't worth living without her.

And it was wasn't worth living knowing he was the one who'd caused her pain. That he'd hurt her.

She hugged him back. "I'm all right, Sten."

He squeezed her and pressed his face to her hair.

A minute ticked by. "We need to get the cart moving again," she murmured.

It was hard, but he managed to loosen his hold. He let go of her, then cleared his throat.

She lifted a hand, and it hovered in the air for a moment. He pushed his face against her fingers, and she ran her fingertips over his jaw.

That small touch steadied him. He turned and focused his attention on the cart controls. "The power's died."

Her mouth flattened. "Do you think the Gek'Dragar will follow?"

"Yes, but at least it won't be easy for them." He swiveled, checking the cart. He grunted and opened a hatch at the back.

"What is it?"

"A manual control." He unfolded a handle, then pushed, then pulled it. The cart inched forward. He started pumping the handle and found a rhythm. It wasn't fast, but they were moving again.

The cart came around a corner.

"Stars," Carys murmured.

A blue waterfall of liquid cascaded from one of the

mine walls. It glowed brightly, part of it falling down over the rail and into the chasm.

"The mining fluid," she breathed.

He cursed. "*Gul*, it's hitting the rail line."

She looked up and sucked in a breath. "You said it eats away at metal more slowly."

"Yes. But we have no idea how long it's been hitting the rail."

"And we need to pass through it."

She tapped a finger against her lips. "I can make an energy shield to deflect the fluid. Then we pass through it as fast as we can."

It wasn't a great idea, but it was the best they had.

He nodded. "Ready?"

She nodded back. "Ready."

She lifted her palms and energy formed, threading together. Sten felt the prickle of power against his skin. A large, blue rectangle of a shield formed on her hands. She thrust it up above their heads. "Go."

Sten worked the crank as fast as he could. She maneuvered close to him, her back pressed to his as she held up the shield. He crouched a little and kept them moving.

They shifted under the waterfall, and the fluid hit the shield. Carys braced. Several small droplets dripped off the metal, hitting the edge of the cart. It sizzled.

Gul. Sten saw the rail was about half the size it should be, partly eaten away.

If it broke...

He pumped his arm faster.

"We're through." She dissolved the shield and grinned.

"And look." He pointed ahead.

A platform appeared out of the darkness. Beyond it, lay a tunnel entrance.

"Thank the knights," she said. "I've had enough of this ride."

All of a sudden, the cart lurched to the side, tilting wildly.

They both grabbed onto the seats and sides of the cart.

It was slanted on its side. Sten looked down at the yawning darkness below and gritted his teeth.

"Sten, the rail line isn't going to hold much longer." Her tone was low and urgent.

They had to hurry.

"Get into the front of the cart and get ready to jump." He cranked the handle, and the tilted cart moved, metal screeching on metal.

She climbed up and perched on the front of the cart.

"Almost there," he said. "Go!"

She leaped into the air, athletic and graceful. She landed on the platform with a roll.

There was a crack from overhead.

Sten felt the cart dip.

His luck had run out.

It was too far to jump from the back of the cart. If he moved, the cart would fall.

Suddenly, there was another screech, and the cart fell away from under his feet.

"Sten!" Carys' scream echoed through the chasm.

He leaped straight up, using all his enhanced strength.

His hand closed around the main rail. He held on tight and looked down.

The falling cart was swallowed by the darkness.

Leaving him dangling.

CHAPTER NINE

"Sten!"

Carys' heart pounded. She ignored the car dropping away; instead, she watched Sten dangling from the broken rail line.

"I'm okay," he said.

But he wasn't. It was too far for him to jump to the platform.

"Can you climb along the rail and come across?" she asked.

"There's some of that blue fluid on the line. If I touch the main rail..."

It would eat into his skin.

Her belly clenched tight. They needed a plan.

She *wasn't* losing him.

Carys searched around the platform, but it was empty.

"The fluid will break through the main rail line soon." His voice was calm.

Panic fluttered through her.

They had no idea how long they had.

"Hold on," she said.

"No." His voice was deep, with that infuriating unruffled tone. "Carys, you need to go. Get help. Get away from here, and find a way to contact Oron."

Her head snapped up. "And leave you?"

"You're the knightqueen. Your life is more important."

She stepped forward, her throat tight. "Yours is important, too."

"Carys—"

"It's important to *me*." She glared at him across the gap. "Now, hold on."

She swiveled and raced out into the tunnel. She would save the irritating man, if it was the last thing she did.

She hurried along, her pulse racing. She knew that any second, he could fall.

Before long, she came to a doorway. When she reached it, she paused. There was a tall skeleton lying on the ground, empty eye sockets staring straight ahead. She stepped carefully over it.

Inside the room, she yanked open warped and weathered cupboard doors, searching through the shelves. A cloud of dust made her cough.

Come on. There had to be something she could use to save Sten. Her heart squeezed. She couldn't lose him.

He may not want her the way she wanted him, but he'd been hers a long time.

Her hands touched a coil of rope and her heart leaped. *Yes.*

She grabbed it and ran.

When she got back to the chasm, he was still hanging there.

"Carys, go." His voice was a growl. "Get yourself safe. That's what's most important to me."

"Save your breath, Thorsten." She hefted the rope. "Get ready to grab this."

His gaze bored into hers. "I'm too heavy. I'll pull you over the edge."

"Then I have another order for you. I order you to catch this rope. I *will* get you over here. Do you understand, Knightguard?"

He glared. "Yes," he said through gritted teeth.

Carys threw the rope.

He caught the end with one hand, still dangling from the rail line with his other one.

She nodded, gripping her end of the rope firmly. "Good now—"

The rail line broke.

He plummeted.

His full weight hit the rope and yanked her forward.

No.

She gripped the rope with all her strength and formed her sword in her other hand. She rammed the end of the blade into the platform. She needed an anchor. The ground sizzled when pure energy met rock.

Her shoulder wrenched as she took Sten's full weight, pain sizzling through her. She gritted her teeth.

"Sten?" she said, strained.

"I'm all right." His voice filtered up from the chasm.

She heard the sound of rocks falling, then a tug on

the rope. A second later, he climbed over the edge of the platform.

Relief and elation hit her. With the strain gone, she let go of the rope and collapsed. Her sword dissolved in an instant.

He dropped down beside her, panting.

"You are so stubborn," he bit out.

"So are you." She rolled into his body. His warmth hit her, and she shivered. He was alive. *Thank the knights*.

He reached up and rubbed her sore shoulder. "You should've left me."

She lifted her chin. "You're mine, Thorsten. I will never leave you." She leaned over him and cupped his chin. "Because I love you."

Shock made his green eyes go wide.

Her insides trembled. Oh, had she just blurted that out loud?

Blurted out her deepest, most secret feelings for a man who'd only kissed her because she'd ordered him to?

She fought back the hot mix of emotions, embarrassment leading the way.

You're the Knightqueen of Oronis. Act like it.

She pushed to her feet, setting her shoulders back, and dusted herself off. She did her best to lock down her rioting emotions.

"I know you don't feel the same, that you don't want me the way I want you. But it doesn't change my feelings. Don't worry, I won't demand anything from you." She nodded, pretending like her insides weren't twisted into a hundred painful knots. "Now, we need to get out of this mine. Are you ready?"

He rose in a lithe move for such a big man. He was still staring at her. "I'm ready."

"Good." She walked off the platform and into the tunnel like a queen.

Not like a woman who'd just bared her vulnerable heart to the man she loved.

SHE COULDN'T MEAN IT.

Because I love you.

Sten felt like someone had hit him in the head as he followed Carys through the tunnel. He couldn't quite get his brain working properly.

Knightqueen Carys couldn't be in love with him. Him? A battle-scarred guard? He wasn't worthy of her. There was no way he could sit beside her. He wasn't king material.

She couldn't mean it.

"Sten, look there's light."

He saw the glow ahead, and followed her. She'd risked herself to save him. She was so selfless, beautiful, and kind.

She looked so slim and lithe in her black armor. It slicked over her body, and at least now she had some shoes on her feet.

They reached the crumbled entrance and stepped out into sunlight.

The ocean was closer; the air held a tang of salt. The landscape was different, as well. Less rugged. The giant mountains had softened into rolling hills. There were fewer rocks, and more vegetation. Ahead lay a field of deep-green grass, dotted with multicolored flowers.

"Let's head that way." Carys set off at a quick pace.

His gaze dropped to her long legs, and desire stabbed him in the gut.

You're mine, Thorsten.

I will never leave you.

Because I love you.

As the words echoed in his head, his chest tightened. He hated feeling this strange mix of confusion and need.

Such a fierce need for her.

He'd been fighting to keep all his feelings for her locked away for so long. For years, he'd never, ever let himself put a name to them.

He knew very little about love. His mother had died when he was a boy, and he only had vague memories of gentle hugs and soft laughter. His father had been a simple, gruff man. He'd been a good father, but they'd never talked about their feelings.

Once Sten had joined the academy to train as a knight, his life had been about strength and training to be the best. Weakness had no place in a knightguard's life. And emotions made you vulnerable.

But his and Carys' abduction at the hands of the Gek'Dragar and everything they'd been through on this planet had left him with weakened defenses.

His chest heaved. They trekked in silence, following a rough path that led up a hill. He scanned the landscape, but there was thankfully no sign of the Gek'Dragar.

"You don't love me." The words were torn out of him.

Carys slowed and whirled. Her hands clenched at

her sides. She strode up to him, pink in her cheeks, then poked him in the chest.

"You do *not* get to tell me what I'm feeling or not feeling, Thorsten."

"Carys—"

She poked him again. "No."

"This is a dangerous, emotional situation—"

She growled. "Yes, and it's made things clear to me. We could've died numerous times. Life is short, and you shouldn't hide things." Her gold eyes were angry. "I love you. I've loved you for years. You're strong and certain and loyal. You've always been there for me." She bit her lip. "And you're tall and rugged and…" Her gaze drifted down his body.

He sucked in a breath.

"These are my feelings." Her chin lifted. "You can ignore them, you can ignore this, but it won't change how I feel. I know you don't feel the same. I know you only kissed me because I ordered you to, not because you truly want me." There was a flash of pain on her face, but she held his gaze. So proud and regal. "I know everything you do is because of your dedication and duty. So don't worry. I won't get confused again." She gave him a brisk nod. "Now, let's go."

She turned and continued to walk down the path.

Sten stared after her. His fingers curled into fists and his chest was rising and falling fast.

Carys thought he didn't desire her? Didn't have feelings for her beyond his job?

He stomped after her.

"We'll continue to the ocean. Find a village—"

He grabbed her arm and spun her around.

She gasped.

"Any man who didn't desire you would have to be dead."

Her lips pressed together. "I don't care about other men."

Sten felt something snap inside him. He dragged in a deep breath, then scooped her into his arms.

"Sten!"

He took two steps and pinned her against a nearby rock. Her hands gripped his shoulders.

"I want you so much that sometimes it hurts," he growled.

Her lips parted.

"From the moment I met you, I thought you were the most beautiful woman in the galaxy. When you were younger, that was just a fact. As you got older..." He swallowed. "I noticed in different ways. Then, I also learned that you are kind and fair, and dedicated to your people. I've watched you grow into a good ruler and a wonderful queen." He swallowed. "A gorgeous woman who's funny and smart and thoughtful." He leaned his forehead against hers. "Who looks mouthwatering in her gowns or her armor. Who takes my breath away. Every day."

"You've never said this much all at once." Her breathing quickened, her eyes wide.

"Every day I fight to hide what I feel for you. Every night, alone in my bed, I stroke myself thinking of you."

Her cheeks flushed and her fingers flexed on his shoulders.

"Every time I see some handsome man ask you to

dance at a party, or touch your hand, or try to get your attention, I have to stop myself from ripping their arms off."

"Sten?"

"Yes?"

"Kiss me."

He shuddered. "As my queen commands."

Her fingers dug into his muscles. "No. Because you want to."

"Let me show you how much I want you." Sten pressed his mouth to hers.

The kiss started gentle. A tantalizing brush of their lips. But it didn't take long before it turned wild, heated. He thrust his tongue between her lips, and she kissed him back, her body rubbing against his. The taste of her was like an explosion of the finest flavors.

She melted into him, her tongue hot and eager against his. He let his mouth drift lower, over her jaw, down her neck. Her skin was like the finest silk.

"Please, touch me," she panted.

"You have no idea the things I want to do to you. All the places I want to touch you."

"*Sten.*"

He couldn't deny her anything. "Retract your armor, Carys."

She did, the black armor withdrawing. He slid his hands under her skirts, his palms cupping her taut ass.

With a gasp, she locked her legs around him.

She reached down and tugged the front of her dress. Her breasts spilled out. "Touch me. Any way you want."

With a groan, he closed his mouth over one nipple.

"*Oh.*" Her hips moved against him.

He sucked firmly. "Do you like that?" he asked against her skin.

"*Yes.*" Her hot gaze met his.

He growled. Need was heavy in his gut. He slid his hand between her legs, and found that she was already wet. He stroked, savoring her warmth and softness.

She arched and let out a small cry.

"Dreamed of touching you here." He found the small, swollen nub at the top of her sex and rubbed. She made a husky sound and jerked. "Dreamed of kissing you here."

More heat flooded her cheeks. "It feels so good. I ache so much. For you."

He groaned, stroking her harder. But while they were partially concealed in the shadow of the hillside, he was still vitally aware that they were in the open, and being hunted.

The knightguard in him warned him to keep moving, to find safety. The man in him saw the desperate desire on her face. It made something twist inside him.

"Please, Sten," she implored. "Show me..."

He couldn't leave her hurting and unfulfilled.

He shoved his thigh between her legs, putting pressure where he knew she needed it. She let out a small cry.

"That's right, Carys." With his hands on her hips, he urged her to move.

She rubbed against him, her eyes glazed. "That feels so good. Stars, please, Sten."

"I know, sweetness. Now, I want you to come for me."

She rocked faster, her breathing thickening. "*Sten.*"

"Soon, when we're safe, I'm going to put my mouth between your legs. Lick you until you come."

She cried out.

"Then I'll slide my cock inside you. It'll be tight, you'll feel it, but I'll make it so good for you."

A desperate sob escaped her, and she slid her hand into his hair, tugged. He knew she was close. Knowing he was making her feel good made his chest swell. She was his to protect, and to take care of, in all ways.

"Come, Carys. On me, for me."

She clamped down on his thick thigh, moving sinuously, searching for more friction. He cupped her ass, and then she stiffened and shattered.

And Sten got to see the most beautiful sight he'd ever known—Carys finding her pleasure.

CHAPTER TEN

Oh, she felt good.

Carys sagged against Sten, but he held her with ease. She should probably be embarrassed. She'd just rubbed against him like a *taurline* cat in heat.

It didn't matter. She felt too good, and was too relaxed, to dredge up any embarrassment.

He tipped her chin up. Desire was clearly written on his rugged face.

"Beautiful," he murmured. "I like watching you come."

She blushed. *Stars*. He made her feel young and giddy, but he also made her feel like a woman.

He let her slide down his body until her feet hit the ground.

"Anymore doubt about how much I want you?" he asked.

She bit her lip. "No."

"Good." He pressed a firm kiss to her mouth. "When we're safe, I'll show you more."

She shivered.

He gripped her chin. "Carys, I'm done fighting this. We take this any further and you're mine."

In her chest, her heart tripped and picked up speed.

"There will be no handsome princes or self-important aristocrats."

She pressed a palm flat against his chest. "I want *you*, Sten. I love you."

Emotion crossed his face. "I—"

Then a buzzing sound suddenly caught their attention.

Sten stiffened and turned, covering her. Her protective knightguard. She sidestepped him, reforming her armor.

A Gek'Dragar scout ship hovered in the distance.

Carys huffed out a breath. "They never give up."

He grunted. "It's not coming this way, but we need to move."

She nodded.

He squeezed her hand.

They set off down the path at a punishing pace. She pumped her arms, falling into a good rhythm. Beside her, Sten adjusted his longer strides to match hers.

Soon, they were over the top of the hill, and the sound of the ship faded behind them. They moved into a meadow of flowers that were white and fragrant.

"Let's take a short break," he said.

She crouched down and picked a flower.

Sten sat beside her. "Pretty."

"It is." She stuck it behind her ear.

"Not as pretty as *verlorna* lilies."

"My favorite. My maids make sure I have a fresh vase of them every week in my room."

Sten looked away and shifted. "That's nice."

She eyed him, and realization filtered through her. "*You*. You leave the lilies."

He shrugged one broad shoulder. "They're your favorite."

"Sten, are you blushing?"

"I don't blush," he said gruffly.

Delight filled her. She leaned in and kissed his cheek. She could touch him. She could kiss him anytime she wanted. The realization made her dizzy.

She wished they weren't in danger. She wished she had time to indulge. She'd give anything for them to be in her bedroom at the palace. Her big bed would easily fit his large frame.

She scanned his chest. She wanted to explore every part of his muscular body.

He grabbed her hand and squeezed. "We can't linger any longer. Can you go on?"

She sighed and nodded. "Yes, of course."

He helped her up, and they set off across the meadow.

He scowled. "There's not much cover here."

"But we'll hear them coming."

He still didn't look happy. They crossed the meadow, and moved back into the rock-strewn hills.

"How long until we reach the ocean?" she asked.

"We're still a long way off."

She sighed. Nothing was ever easy.

Then she saw him slow. "Sten?"

He crouched, studying something on the ground. She peered over his shoulder. Footprints. Of something big. Her belly tightened. Something feline, perhaps.

She groaned. "I thought we'd left the monsters behind in the ravines."

He rose, his shoulders tense. "Stay alert."

They headed down a narrow path. They hadn't gone far when a scent reached her. Something gamey, with a musky undertone.

She looked up and saw caves set in the side of the hill.

Then a high-pitched scream sliced through the air.

Carys' heart lodged in her throat. "Is that a child?"

They both broke into a sprint and raced over the rise.

A huge, feline creature, with a muscled, powerful body, and long claws was advancing on a tall child with dark-red skin. The boy's large black eyes contrasted with the white markings on his face.

He looked terrified.

"Sten," Carys said.

He formed his broadsword. "I'll save him." Then he charged down the hill and leaped into the air.

The cat swiveled and snarled.

Carys sprinted down as well, running toward the child.

Sten sliced with his sword. He moved so fast for such a large man. The cat swiped out with its claws, its jaws snapping.

She reached the child.

"Come." She held out a hand.

The boy's eyes were huge and dark. His body shook.

"I won't hurt you."

Then Carys saw a second cat slink out of the shadows of some rocks. The child gasped and ran to her.

She formed her own sword and pushed the child behind her. The boy whimpered.

"I won't let it hurt you." She raised the sword and focused on the incoming predator.

The cat sprang.

Carys moved fast, her blade cutting into fur. Blood spotted the ground. The cat hissed and sprang back.

She changed her grip and watched, her muscles tense.

The cat sprinted forward, but she was ready. She whirled, her blade glowing. She thrust, and rammed it into the cat's side. It yelped.

She yanked the blade free. The cat leaped into the air and Carys dodged. Claws swiped past her, and she felt the strike of them against her armor.

Then a large body landed on the cat's back.

Sten raised his sword and brought it down on the feline's neck.

The beast twisted, but Sten held on. He shoved his sword down with a grunt. It sliced deep, cutting vital things.

The light went out of the beast's eyes. It took a stumbling step, and then its legs collapsed.

Face like stone, Sten pulled his sword free. He leaped off the animal's dead body, landing with a bend of his knees.

He looked like an avenging knight of old, talked about in the old myths.

"Are you all right?" he asked.

She nodded. She looked over at the first cat he'd fought. It was dead as well.

She heard a sob and turned to the child.

"It's okay." Carys held out a hand, letting her sword dissipate. "You're safe now."

The boy hesitated for a second, then he ran straight to her. He threw his arms around her waist.

Oh. She felt him shaking. She stroked his dark hair. She thought he was quite young, but he was taller than an Oronis child, so it was hard to tell.

"You're safe now," she murmured.

Sten stepped in close and touched her cheek.

The boy pulled back, his gaze curious. He looked at their armor and then Sten's sword. As Sten dissolved his weapon, the boy's eyes went wide.

He babbled in a language that her translator didn't understand.

"You get any of that?" she asked Sten.

He shook his head. "His language isn't in our databanks. All right, let's—"

There was a whoosh of noise.

Overhead, a dark Gek'Dragar scout ship swung into view.

Carys' chest locked and she grabbed the boy.

ENERGY SURGED THROUGH STEN. "RUN!"

He shoved Carys. She scooped up the boy and ran. Sten was right behind her.

The scout ship opened fire—laser chasing them across the hillside.

As he ran, Sten pulled energy to him, felt it increasing. His focus narrowed on the ship. He threw an energy ball.

It hit the ship and the vessel jerked.

Carys swiveled, and formed a shield on her arm. She held it up, protecting the child.

Sten spotted what looked like the entrance to some caves up ahead. "We need to reach the caves."

She nodded and picked up speed.

Sprinting, Sten lifted the boy from her arms into his own. He clung to Sten, the red skin on his face looking ashen.

Carys formed an energy bow. She held it up and fired several energy bolts at the ship. The ship returned fire, and they ducked behind some rocks.

The boy curled into a ball and Sten kept him close. "We're pinned down."

More laser fire hit all around them.

Carys ducked lower. "The caves are still too far away."

Sten gritted his teeth, trying to find a way out. The ship's engines whined as it spun around in front of them.

"Protect him." Carys rose and sprinted at the ship.

No. His chest locked. "Carys, stay in cover!"

She jumped on top of a large rock, then leaped into the air. She landed on the wing of the ship, and ran along it.

He watched the Gek'Dragar pilot in the cockpit arching his head, searching for her.

Her sword glowed blue in her hand. When she reached the central part of the ship, she stabbed downward, cutting into the roof. The metal parted like water under the energy blade.

The ship jerked to the left, and Carys lurched.

Sten froze. *Don't fall. Don't fall.*

She didn't. Graceful as ever, she crouched, keeping her balance. Then dropped down into the hole she'd cut and into the ship.

Chest tight, he watched and waited. It should be him up there risking his life, not her.

A moment later, smoke erupted from the back of the scout ship.

"Come on, Carys."

Then he saw her. Relief punched through him. She leaped onto the top of the ship and jumped off. She somersaulted in the air, then hit the ground and rolled.

The damaged scout ship spun in a circle and flew away. More smoke poured from it. Then it careened sideways and smashed into the hillside. It exploded, a ball of flames rising into the sky.

Beside him, the boy made an excited noise and clapped his hands. He grinned at Sten.

"Yes, she's fierce," Sten said.

Carys ran over to them.

"Are you all right?" he barked.

"I'm fine." She looked at the wide-eyed boy. "But that's going to attract attention."

"We'd better move fast."

The boy wiggled to get down. He waved a hand at them and jogged up a path.

Carys shrugged. "Let's follow him. He must know the area."

They followed the boy up the hill. The path twisted and turned, and, without their small guide, they probably would've gotten lost.

Behind them, the sound of more ship engines filled the air.

"Hide," Sten ordered.

They ducked under an outcrop of rocks. The three of them squeezed into the tight space, the boy wedged between them.

Then another Gek'Dragar scout ship flew slowly overhead.

The child trembled.

"It's okay." Carys hugged him to her. "You're not alone."

The boy couldn't understand her, but it appeared her tone soothed him.

"We'll keep you safe," she promised.

Sten stared at the curve of her cheekbone. That was Carys, always looking out for others. Always willing to risk herself to keep others safe.

The ship finally moved on.

Sten blew out a breath. But the Gek'Dragar were here, close by, and looking for them.

He ducked out of their hiding spot. "Come on. We need to move."

They stayed close to the cliff face as they moved farther up the hill.

Shouts echoed from somewhere in the distance. Stars, there were Gek'Dragar soldiers on the ground.

"Sten?"

"We don't have any good cover here." If they crested the hill, they'd be spotted.

The boy suddenly turned left, darting down another path.

Sten saw the walls of rock converged. There was no way out in that direction. "Wait. That's a dead end."

But the boy didn't slow down, just waved at them.

"Do you have a better option?" Carys said. "He must know a way out."

Sten gritted his teeth and set off after the boy. At the end of the path, there was nothing but rock walls.

Swallowing a curse, Sten looked around. If the Gek'-Dragar cornered them here, they'd be trapped.

Then the boy dropped down, crawled forward, and disappeared.

What? Sten and Carys pushed forward.

"Oh, there's a small, concealed tunnel." Carys dropped to her knees. "I didn't even see this. The rocks hide it." Then she pulled a face. "It's small."

Sten studied it. "You'll fit."

She glared up at him. "I'm *not* leaving you."

He blew out a loud breath. "Fine. I'll get through it. You go first."

She crawled in, and his gaze dropped to her ass. He closed his eyes.

"Come on, Sten," she called back.

He crawled into the tunnel. His shoulders brushed the rock on either side. It was a tight squeeze, but he crept forward. "The boy?"

"He's waiting ahead. He wants us to follow him."

Sten crawled on. It was very snug in places, and he had to force his shoulders through.

"There's light ahead," she called back.

He glanced up, but all he could see was his queen's fine ass. Suddenly, his shoulders wedged tight. He cursed.

"What's wrong?" she asked.

"I'm stuck."

"We're almost there."

He tried to shove forward, but his shoulders weren't moving.

"Hang on." She disappeared, then she reappeared face first. "It's just a little farther." She smiled, then pressed a quick kiss to his lips. "Give me your hands."

Sten held his hands out and she entwined their fingers. Then she pulled, her muscles straining.

He moved a tiny bit. She gave another huge yank.

A second later, he broke free, but his shoulders stung as a layer of skin scraped off his shoulders. He cursed.

"Such language, Knightguard Sten," Carys teased.

"Because I'm the one with skin missing."

They crawled out of the tiny tunnel.

Sten rose and froze.

"Oh, no." Carys gripped his hand.

A dozen tall, powerful warriors with red skin were glaring at them, holding bows filled with glowing red bolts.

The boy let out an excited squeal, then ran. He was scooped up by a tall man. He babbled at the man, his hands waving.

Sten stepped in front of Carys.

"Get back in the tunnel," he murmured.

"They'll shoot you."

"Carys—"

The warrior set the child down and patted the boy's head. Then he stepped forward.

"You saved my nephew from the Gek'Dragar."

Sten could understand him. The translator detected his language.

"He's a child." Carys pushed past Sten, looking regal.

He gripped her waist to stop her from moving any closer.

"The Gek'Dragar are our enemy," she continued. "We couldn't let them hurt the boy."

The warrior inclined his head. "Thank you." He studied them, his dark gaze narrowing. "You're Oronis."

"Yes," Carys said.

"We are the Ti-Lore."

"This is your planet?" she asked. "Ti-Lore?"

The man nodded. "There are not many of my people left."

The warrior switched to another language, the one the boy had used, and spoke to the men behind him. The other warriors all lowered their weapons.

Then he looked back at Carys and Sten.

"I am Azulon. Anyone who cares for my family is a friend. Come."

CHAPTER ELEVEN

Sten was watchful as they followed the Ti-Lore warriors.

"They seem friendly," Carys said.

"We'll see."

She hid her smile. Her grumpy and untrusting knightguard.

They followed a well-trodden path through the hills. Carys tensed at the sound of snorting animals.

Ahead, a small herd of goat-like creatures milled, nibbling on the sparse grass growing between the rocks. They were sturdy, with large bodies and huge, curled horns on their heads. They were covered in dense, white fur, and all wore small saddles.

She watched the warriors swing onto their backs.

Sten's frown deepened, and he touched her arm.

"It'll be fine," she said.

Azulon climbed onto one of the creatures and patted in front of him. His nephew scrambled on and then leaned over, stroking the creature's neck.

"We will travel to our village on the *chiru*," Azulon said.

Another warrior led a creature over to them.

"We only have one to spare, but it will safely carry both of your weight."

"Thank you," Carys said.

Sten climbed on. He held out a hand to her and then pulled her up, settling her in front of him. She suppressed a shiver at the feel of his big body behind her.

The creature, the *chiru*, shifted and snorted.

Sten took the reins, then they set off.

Azulon moved his beast up beside theirs. The boy smiled at her.

"My name is Carys," she said to Azulon. "And this is Sten."

The warrior inclined his head.

"And your nephew's name?"

Azulon ruffled his nephew's hair. "Malthor."

"Hello, Malthor," Carys said.

The boy beamed at her.

"It's not far to our village," Azulon said.

They picked up speed, and soon, Carys adjusted to the gait of the animal. Sten's arm was tight around her, and she didn't worry about falling. She leaned back into him.

He nuzzled her head. "You're not injured?"

"I'm fine, Sten. I'm a knight, remember?"

"I know. It doesn't mean I like seeing you risk yourself."

His words ignited a warm glow inside her.

"You did well taking down that scout ship," he said.

The glow increased. "Thanks." She shifted in the saddle, and he groaned. His hand clamped on her hip.

"Stop moving."

"Why?" Her pulse fluttered.

"Because my body is responding to yours. I'm riding an alien animal with a beautiful woman in my lap. I'm hard, and it isn't exactly comfortable."

She tried to look contrite. "Sorry."

He snorted. "No, you're not." He squeezed her hip, then lowered his voice. "It's made worse by the fact that I can't do anything about it right now."

His husky rumble vibrated deep within her. "Would you do something if you could?"

He leaned in, his mouth at her ear. "I can't fight what I feel for you any longer, Carys. I would do whatever my queen demands. Not because of duty. Not because you ordered it. But because all I want is to please you."

Heat coiled in her belly. "*Sten.*"

His palm spread over her belly. "Behave."

"Things will change between us," she said.

"I know."

This time, she didn't hear any hesitation in his voice.

The hills suddenly gave way to a flat plane. Carys glanced back at the forbidding mountains behind them. They weren't free yet, but this felt a step closer.

Her mouth flattened. Then the Gek'Dragar would feel the might of the Oronis.

The glimmer of the ocean got closer, and she saw several small plumes of smoke curling upward.

"That is our village," Azulon said. "Once, we called the mountains home, but then everything changed."

"The Gek'Dragar," she said quietly.

The Ti-Lore nodded. "The Gek'Dragar."

The *chiru* walked on, the warriors murmuring between themselves. The path widened and the settlement came into view.

All the buildings were circular huts with domed roofs. They were made from bricks and some sort of woven straw. Colorful fabric flapped on lines strung between buildings.

Women, men, and children came out to greet them. They were all tall and lean, with dark-red skin and black hair, and wearing clothes with touches of fur. Most of the Ti-Lore were young. There were some elders, but not many.

The kids ran alongside the *chiru*. Some were scooped up by warriors.

"They're a peaceful people." She felt so much sorrow for them. "Their world and way of life have been destroyed by the Gek'Dragar."

"They're survivors. They haven't let it warp them."

The *chiru* stopped in the center of the village. Carys saw the villagers shoot her and Sten curious looks. Sten swung off the animal, then gripped her waist and lifted her down.

She saw Azulon talking to a woman with long, silky, black hair. The white markings on her face ran up her cheeks and were more delicate than those on the men. Then Malthor ran toward her, and she hugged the boy hard.

Then the woman looked up and caught Carys' gaze. "Thank you for helping my son."

Carys nodded. "It was our pleasure. And he helped us in return."

"Carys, Sten," Azulon said, "this is my sister, Nythoria."

"How did you come to Ti-Lore?" Nythoria asked.

"As prisoners of the Gek'Dragar," Carys answered.

A rumble of exclamation ran through the villagers. The woman's eyes widened. "You escaped their prison?"

Carys nodded. "Yes."

Azulon stepped forward. "It was you who destroyed it?"

"Not us." Sten shook his head. "We just escaped in the chaos of the attack."

"You're lucky to be alive," the other man said. "The mountains are unstable, and filled with twisted creatures."

"We know," Sten said. "We fought our way out. What happened here on your planet?"

Nythoria's face twisted. "The Gek'Dragar ruined our mountains, our villages, and our animals."

Azulon's face hardened. "The Gek'Dragar used our *plorion*."

"The blue mining fluid?" Carys said.

Azulon nodded. "For centuries, my people had used it in small amounts. We controlled its use." His jaw tightened. "But the Gek'Dragar overused it. It destroyed our mountains, warped the animals."

His sister leaned into him, and he hugged her.

"I'm sorry," Carys said. "We must find a way to return to Oron. We need a communicator, or some way to contact our people. We have to stop the Gek'Dragar. I suspect that they're planning to attack our planet too."

"No one can stop them," Nythoria said.

"Knightqueen Carys can," Sten stated.

"Knightqueen?" Azulon froze. "You are the Queen of Oron?"

Carys nodded.

The man bowed his head. "You are so welcome among us, Knightqueen."

"Thank you, Azulon. Please, no need to bow. We're grateful for your help."

"Do you have a communicator?" Sten asked.

Azulon shook his head. "We do not have a communications device here."

Carys' shoulders sagged.

"But the head of a neighboring village has some technology. He managed to hide it when our villages in the mountains fell. I will contact him, and see if he can help."

Hope surged through her. "Thank you."

Nythoria smiled. "I'm sure you would like to bathe, and change into some fresh clothes." She eyed them. "We will need to adjust some of our clothes to fit you."

Azulon nodded. "Nythoria can see to whatever you need. I will let you know when I hear from the neighboring village."

"Come," Nythoria said, waving a hand.

Carys took Sten's hand and followed the woman into the village.

THE FEMALE TI-LORE led them to one of the round-topped buildings. She smiled, and waved them inside.

"Oh, this is beautiful," Carys said.

The interior was covered in a plush rug, with vibrant wall hangings. A bed of overstuffed pillows sat to one side. Walking to the nearest wall hanging, she fingered the exquisite stitching.

Nythoria smiled. "Thank you. Our way of life has changed, but we've tried our best to adapt and not lose our skills. Making fabric and stitching our art onto it is a time-honored tradition." She pushed back a dark-red wall hanging. "This is the way to your adjoining private bath house. We have natural mineral springs here."

A wash of steam rolled over Sten. A second, round building with no windows was attached to the first. Inside was a large, irregular-shaped pool, with steam rising off the water.

"Hello? I have food for our guests." An older Ti-Lore man entered the main hut, carrying a platter. He was tall and lean, but there was gray threaded in his long, black hair. Sten noticed he also had a heavy limp.

The tray was covered in fruits and breads, and a creamy-looking soup. There was also a glass bottle filled with red liquid. He set it down on a table.

"Thank you, Rinkin," Nythoria said.

Carys smiled at the man. "Yes, thank you."

He bowed his head. "My pleasure, Knightqueen." He left quietly.

"Rest, Knightqueen." Nythoria nodded to her and Sten. "It will take time for our messenger to reach the neighboring village. We will not hear news before morning."

"Thank you again, Nythoria," Carys said.

"You saved my son. You never have to thank me." She left with a swish of her skirts.

"We can bathe." Carys whirled around, excitement stamped all over her face. "*Finally*." Her armor retracted, leaving her barefoot in her tattered dress.

His gut clenched at the thought of her naked. "You go ahead."

She straightened. "No, we're both bathing." She grabbed his hand and dragged him into the bath house.

The air was warm, but he knew it wasn't just the humidity. It was the desire that had remained a constant, low simmer inside him.

"Oh, look. There are soaps and lotions." She gestured at a tray resting beside the hot pool.

He grunted. Soap was the last thing on his mind right now.

Control. He needed some control. The intensity of his desire for this woman was beyond anything he'd experienced. And she'd never been with a man. He didn't want to hurt her.

She spun to face him. "I can hear you thinking, Sten."

"I—"

"No." She held up a hand. "We're safe for now. It's time to stop thinking."

Then, before he realized what she had planned, she reached over her shoulder to the fastening of her dress. A second later, the fabric pooled at her feet.

He sucked in a breath.

His brain wouldn't work. She was so beautiful. A long, slender body with gentle curves. Elegant, feminine, with pale-gold skin. She slid her underwear off and met his gaze, her chin lifted. She turned and strode into the water.

His gaze dropped to her ass. Those sweet globes.

When she was in the water, she turned. Her breasts bobbed, the upper curves pulling his gaze.

His throat was so tight he could barely breathe, and desire was heavy in his gut. In his thickening cock.

"You're incredibly beautiful, Carys."

She blushed. "You are, too."

He snorted. "I'm a knightguard. I'm rough, and big, and scarred."

"Beautiful in a masculine way. Your size and scars show your strength." Her gaze locked on his. "Take your clothes off, Thorsten."

He hesitated.

"Your queen commands it." Her tone was low and playful.

He shuddered. The need for her was so strong. He wanted to stride into the pool and pull her into his arms.

To finally indulge everything he'd ever fantasized about this woman.

He yanked his shirt off, then unfastened his trousers.

He'd never given his body much thought before, except that it was fit, muscular, and strong for doing his job. But he was well-aware he was big and scarred, not handsome and elegant like the men Carys entertained at her gatherings and balls.

As he kicked his trousers away, there was no hiding his hard cock. He straightened. Carys was staring at him, her gaze running over his body.

Desire was etched on her face.

"You're so strong, Sten."

He pulled in a breath.

She moved to the edge of the pool, tantalizingly close. His cock rose to his abdomen.

"All of you is big and strong." She glanced down at the water. "It reminds me of when I watched you. In the mine." She looked up, her cheeks flushed. "When you stroked yourself and said my name. I was so wet. I wanted so much to touch you."

He sucked in a sharp breath.

"Stroke yourself now. Show me. Show your queen."

He groaned and circled his cock roughly. Her lips parted.

Having her watch him... He bit off the curse and pumped. He gripped himself harder, stroked faster.

"*Sten*." She was entranced.

"It's hard for you," he growled.

"Come here."

He staggered into the pool, and she rose to meet him. Her slick skin brushed him, and he clenched his muscles, stopping himself from coming.

"I want to touch you," she murmured. "I want to help you."

Then his queen, the woman he'd wanted for years, wrapped her elegant hands around his cock beside his.

"This part of you is not how I imagined," she said. "It's hard and strong like steel, but the skin is so soft."

Her finger traced up an engorged vein running up his cock.

His hips jerked, shoving his cock into her soft palm.

"Show me how to touch you," she murmured.

He helped her stroke him. His gaze dropped to her breasts, her pretty, pink nipples. A gruff rumble broke from him.

"Harder." His voice was like grit.

Carys leaned in, stroking harder. She tightened her grip on him.

He dropped his head and kissed her.

She kissed him back eagerly, and together they stroked his cock. Desire clamped down on Sten's spine. Pleasure was building like a storm.

His control was all gone. He was hers. Always.

"*Carys.*" A tortured groaned.

"Come for me, Sten." Her other hand dropped lower and cupped his balls. "Show me."

He had to obey.

His release hit hard, and he heard her gasp. With a groan, his come splashed his skin, her hand, her belly. The force of his release made his back arch. *So good.* His lungs were working like bellows, and it was all he could do to stay upright.

Gul. All Carys had to do was touch him and he came like an untried teenager.

Carys rubbed his seed between her fingers. Then she lifted her hand to her lips and tasted it.

Sten groaned, and tugged her into the pool. "You unman me."

She wrapped her arms around his shoulders. "You look very manly to me."

There was happiness on her face, and Sten realized how happy that made him. "Your turn now." He stroked his thumb over her lips. "Now, I'll take care of you."

CHAPTER TWELVE

Sten's hard body felt so good pressed against hers.

A tremor ran through Carys. She could touch him, all over. Explore his body how she'd dreamed so many times.

She let her hands roam over his thick biceps and shoulders, kneading his amazing muscles.

He held her closer and sank deeper into the water. Then he swam over to the edge where the woven tray sat, filled with a number of small bottles and vials. He pulled the lid off one bottle, and the scent of flowers wafted into the air. He tipped some of the liquid into his big, callused hands, and ran them over her body.

His hands ran down her arms, and back. Then down her sides, across her belly. Each stroke made her insides melt. It was so nice not to smell of dirt and perspiration.

In here, with steam rising in the air, nothing existed but the two of them.

"Hair, next," he murmured.

She tipped her head back. He worked some lotion

into her hair, then massaged her scalp. She closed her eyes, floating in the water. Her big, strong guard was taking care of her.

He could be sweet as well as tough.

He carefully rinsed out her hair.

"My turn." She found soap with a woody scent, and ran it over his chest. She paused at some of the scars marking his skin. There weren't many. An Oronis knight's implants normally healed their wounds, and they rarely left a scar, but these had been from that terrible *nelok* attack. The alien creature had slashed his face and chest, but he'd shielded her for two days. During that time, the wounds had become infected. She reached up and traced the scars on his cheek.

"They aren't pretty," he said.

"They're a sign of your courage and bravery."

"I'd do anything to keep you safe."

Heat curled in her belly. She stroked her fingers up the ridges of his abdomen, then reached around the curve of his muscular ass.

He made a low sound. There wasn't any fat on him.

Then she turned her attention to the cock rising out of the water. He was hard again. She ran her soapy hands over him, smiling at his low groan. He was so large and thick. She swallowed. She might be a virgin, but she knew how sex worked.

But she wasn't entirely sure how this would fit inside her. She kept stroking him and set the soap aside.

Sten scooped her up into his arms and carried her out of the pool. He grabbed some drying cloths and strode to the low bed of pillows in the adjoining hut. He set her down and then rubbed the drying cloth over her skin carefully, finally dipping between her legs.

Her lips parted. She felt so sensitive, so needy.

She wanted him so much.

Still damp, he pushed her down on the cushioned softness. She lay on the bed, watching his gaze run over her.

"You steal my breath, Carys. And it isn't just your beautiful body and face. You're beautiful inside, too."

She loved that he saw so much of her. That he liked so much of her.

"I want you to show me everything, Sten."

He knelt beside her and cupped one breast. She gasped. His thumb toyed with her nipple until it was a tight nub. "Whatever you want, I'll give it to you."

Power like she'd never felt flowed through her. "Put your mouth on me."

A faint smile tipped his lips. "With pleasure." He leaned over and sucked her nipple into his mouth.

So much sensation. "Oh yes, stars." She ran her hands through his short hair.

He took his time, using his lips, tongue, and teeth. She pushed into his mouth, then he moved to her other breast.

"You're sensitive here," he murmured.

"*Yes*. I love your mouth." He didn't stop until her nipples were both hard, throbbing points.

He smiled, then moved lower. He pressed kisses to her quivering belly.

"Sten..."

"Let me love you, Carys."

Love. The word thrummed through her.

Then his mouth nuzzled her thigh before he licked her skin. She moaned.

"Spread for me," he growled.

She let her thighs fall apart.

He nuzzled her and groaned. "Carys...your scent. *Gul.*"

Then he looked up her naked body. Her pulse was racing fast, the desire leaving her lightheaded. He gripped one of her thighs and lifted it over his shoulder.

She quivered in anticipation, then his hot mouth pressed her slick folds.

A garbled cry escaped her. Her hands clenched on his head.

He used his tongue, lapping at her. Tasting her. His big hands slid underneath her and clenched on her ass. He took his time to taste and tease her. Eating her like a starving man.

She couldn't stay still, pleasure growing inside her. Her moans filled the hut.

His tongue found the small, swollen nub at the top of her, and she bucked. She ground herself against his mouth. He licked and sucked until she was sobbing.

Then, she felt the tip of his finger press against her tight opening. She bit her lip, then he slid it deep.

She moaned. "*Yes.*"

"No one's ever touched you here." His voice was low, growly. "You're so tight and wet."

"Deeper," she pleaded.

He continued licking and sucking, sliding his thick finger deep. When he pushed a second finger inside her, she felt the stretch. She wanted more. She ground against his hand and mouth.

"I can feel you clamping down on my fingers. My cock is bigger, Carys. You'll feel me when I'm inside you."

Just the thought of him inside her, joining them, made everything more intense. "Sten, I'm..."

"Come, my queen."

She imploded with a sharp cry. Her vision blurred, the intense pleasure pulsing through her. Her spine arched and she wound her leg around his broad back.

When she came back to reality, her chest was heaving. Pleasure still shimmered through her.

Sten knelt between her legs, his lips glistening. Her belly contracted.

Heat and need were on his face, glowing in his green eyes.

Reflected in his hard erection.

It was dark and thick, fluid gleaming on the swollen head.

She held out a hand to him.

He hesitated.

"I'm not your queen now, Thorsten. I'm just a woman asking the man she loves to touch her. To be with her and show her pleasure, and take his own pleasure in return."

He made a deep sound, then covered her body with his. He was so hard. Pure muscle.

He nudged her thighs apart with his. She felt small, but not scared. She was never scared with Sten.

He kissed her roughly.

Then she felt his hand between her thighs. He stroked her and she gasped. The head of his cock rubbed along her folds.

Her hips surged up. *Yes. Right there.*

"Patience," he said. "I'm big, and you're not."

"I need you inside me. *Now.*"

With a groan, the head of his cock nudged her folds, and he sank inside her the smallest amount.

She gripped his biceps and felt a flush of nerves.

"You can take me." His voice was guttural.

"I know." She bit his jaw. "Make me yours, Sten. I want to belong to you."

His jaw was tight. He was still fighting for control. He was always caring for her.

"Don't hold back, Sten."

"I've wanted you forever." He thrust forward, lodging his cock deep inside her.

She let out a sharp cry, felt a brief sting of pain. But then it was replaced by a deep ache. The sensation of being stretched and full.

Sten was inside her.

Filling her.

Joining them.

"Carys, sweetness," he panted. "Stars. So tight, warm."

"Don't you dare hold back." She wrapped her legs around his hips, digging her heels into his ass.

"Don't...want to hurt you."

"You won't. You never will."

His hips pulled back, and he started thrusting in a quick, solid rhythm.

She held on, her body shuddering as he moved inside her. He hitched one of her thighs higher up on his side. Now there was no discomfort, only pleasure.

Sten was taking her—rough and hard. Claiming her. Like a warrior taking his hard-earned war prize.

He drove into her relentlessly and they both groaned. He leaned back a little, then pinned her hands above her head with one of his. His gaze ran down her naked body, to where his cock was lodged inside her.

"*Gul*, you fit me just right. Clenched around me so tight."

"You fit me just right," she breathed. "Thick and hard, filling me up."

His eyes squeezed shut. He pulled back, then thrust deep. "My Carys. My Queen. *Mine.*"

She cried out, the force of the sensations building inside her felt a little scary.

Then she felt his hand rub between their bodies where his thick cock thrust inside her. He found her clit.

"My Sten," she gasped. "My guard. *Mine.*"

He groaned, his head bending forward, his eyes glazed.

"Come now." Her voice was breathy. "Come inside me."

There was a blaze of heat on his face, and his thrusts gained speed.

Her climax hit in a blinding rush. She screamed his name and turned her head, biting down on his forearm. Hot pleasure drenched her like a wave.

Sten's body jerked. "Can feel you. All of you."

His final thrust was brutal and deep. He left his cock

deep inside her and groaned her name. She felt a pulse of wet warmth inside her as he came.

HE'D BEEN awake for a while.

Sten had slept well for several hours, but the knight-guard in him kept waking to check that everything was okay in the village.

That Carys was safe.

Plus, he liked savoring the feel of holding a naked, sleeping, and satiated Carys in his arms.

She was sprawled over him, and he stroked her blonde, silky hair.

He'd made love to Carys.

Several times.

He wasn't good enough for her, but he'd done his best to cherish her. He'd made her come over and over again, until she'd been exhausted.

She stirred. Her hand flexed on his chest. Then she looked up and gave him a brilliant smile.

Her happiness made his gut tight.

"Good morning," he said.

"Good morning." She kissed his chest. Of course, his cock stood up and took notice.

"You slept well."

She met his gaze. "I did, but that wasn't a question. You already knew I slept well. Did you stay up all night?"

"I got some sleep." He'd been trained to only need a few naps here and there. He ran his hands over her body. "Sore?"

"No. You know I heal fast." She pressed a kiss to the center of his chest. "I'm going to explore now, Sten. I want to explore you."

He gritted his teeth. He was a trained knight. He could survive this. "Okay."

In that moment, he forgot all about finding a communicator and getting home to Oron. There was only Carys.

She took her time caressing his chest, playing with his flat nipples. Then her mouth and hands traveled lower. With one finger, she traced the ridges of his stomach. She pushed the sheet away and his cock sprang free.

He was already stiff and hurting. He watched her face. Her excitement, desire, and curiosity.

She was going to kill him.

She circled his cock, and his muscles froze. He shifted restlessly on the bed.

"No. Stay still. Reach up and grip the pillows."

He reached up and sank his fingers in the pillows. He was stretched out for her. For his queen. "I'm yours, Carys."

"I know." She smiled. "I'm not sure you truly believe that yet." She stroked his cock again, then lowered her head. "I want to taste you. Take you in my mouth."

Stars. Every muscle in his body locked.

Then she licked his cock, and several curses echoed through his head. She made a humming sound and closed her mouth over him.

His hips surged up, and he heard her cough. But she didn't pull back. Her hand gripped the base of his cock and her mouth moved lower. She sucked hard and squeezed.

"Sweetness..." He groaned. "Your mouth... I—"

She sucked harder and faster. Sten felt his cock swell.

"*Carys*," he growled, sinking a hand into her hair. "I'm not coming in your mouth."

She sat up, licking her lips. "Next time?"

He yanked her over his body.

She straddled his hips, surprise on her face. She pressed her hands to his chest. "Oh, I like this."

He'd had the honor of watching her grow from an intelligent but unsure young queen into the smart, competent knightqueen she was today. She regularly presided over meetings with kings and queens, and planetary leaders. She commanded respect.

It was easy to forget that she was innocent in some ways, as well.

But as she shimmied her hips, all he saw was desire and curiosity on that beautiful face.

"You want to ride my cock, my queen?"

Her cheeks went pink. "Yes."

She lifted her hips, and he helped her position his cock where they both wanted it. The fat head of his cock breached her, and she gasped. He held still as she sank down.

He groaned.

Her lips parted, pleasure on her face. Her nails dug into his chest.

"Now ride." He gripped her hips and urged her on.

She started rising and falling. "Like this?"

By the knights. His control was the barest thread. "Yes." He squeezed her hips. Her breasts were rising and falling fast, and she hovered over his body with eyes filled with heated desire.

Carys rocked her hips, making a husky sound. "You're so deep inside me."

He felt her inner muscles squeeze his cock and bit off a curse. "Feel good? Only you make me this hard."

She made a hungry sound. He reached forward and found her clit.

She gasped and leaned down, biting his lip. Their bodies strained against each other, and he loved how connected they were.

He was joined with Carys.

She rocked her hips, trying different angles. They were both slick with perspiration.

Then she whimpered. "Help me."

"My beautiful queen." He cupped her ass and squeezed. Then he used his strength to lift her up, then thrust her back down. He worked her up and down on his aching cock.

She was panting, her eyes glazed, and he knew she was close.

He skimmed one hand into her hair and tugged. "Come, Carys. I want to watch you. Ride my cock until you come."

She tossed her head back, crying out his name.

His name on her lips when he was deep inside her... It was his darkest fantasy come true.

Sten felt a wild need fill him. *Claim. Claim. Claim.*

He surged up and spun her, knocking her onto her hands and knees.

He ignored her gasp and gripped her hips. His gaze

locked on the sweet curve of her ass. He pushed her legs apart, pressed a rough palm to her lower back, then plunged home.

With a cry, she thrust back against him. "*Sten, please...*"

He savagely drove into her. "I want you to come again."

She made an inarticulate sound, her hands twisting on the pillows. Then she was coming again, her inner muscles clenching on his hard cock.

He couldn't hold back. With a curse, he slammed deep, and his release poured out of him. He grunted and ground against her. "*Carys.*"

When she sagged, he caught her. Air sawed in and out of his lungs. He felt drugged.

He laid her out on the pillows and dropped down beside her.

She shot him a sleepy smile. "I *really* liked that."

His heart squeezed. "Me, too."

She snuggled into him. Burrowing close. "Right here. This is where I feel the best." She breathed in his skin. "The safest."

Sten lay beside her, holding her close. He absorbed her warmth, and the knowledge of how much she trusted him. He buried his face in her hair.

I'll keep you safe. Whatever it takes.

CHAPTER THIRTEEN

The next morning, Carys smiled at the women in the village. They were all a full head taller than her, with long bodies and interesting white markings on their faces. Every person's markings were a little different, but from what she could tell, they appeared to be natural, not a tattoo.

One woman brought her a drape of colorful fabric in a brilliant blue.

"Thank you, it's beautiful."

The woman nodded shyly.

Carys was dressed in clothes similar to the women, with long skirts and a fitted, sleeveless top. It was clear that they were children's clothes that had been altered to fit her.

She spotted Sten talking with Azulon and some other Ti-Lore men and women. He was deep in discussion with them.

A child shyly came forward and handed Carys a red flower.

She smiled and touched the girl's hand.

Then Nythoria arrived, smiling. "You look...well-rested." The Ti-Lore woman shot a glance at Sten.

Carys fought back a blush. "I slept very well."

"I see how much your man makes you happy. And the way he looks at you..." Nythoria's smile turned sad. "It makes me miss my mate."

"You lost him?" Carys touched the other woman's arm. "I'm so sorry."

"I miss him every day. Malthor was still growing inside me when the Gek'Dragar killed Jalaron."

Sorrow wrapped around Carys' throat. "I promise you, Nythoria, I *will* stop the Gek'Dragar. I will make them pay for all the suffering they've caused."

The other woman took Carys' hand and squeezed hard. "I believe you. You're strong, you have a strong man at your side, and I suspect your people won't hesitate to follow you."

"Yes. And we have powerful allies as well."

"I wish I could join you in battle." Nythoria's gaze moved to her son who was running around with the other children. "You will have my prayers."

"And one day, I will return here, when Ti-Lore is a free planet once more," Carys said fiercely.

Nythoria nodded. Then there was a commotion as several Ti-Lore rode in on *chiru*.

Carys' pulse skipped.

"They are from the neighboring village," Nythoria said. "Go. Your man is watching you very intently."

Carys looked up and saw Sten looking her way, his brow creased. As she crossed to him, her belly fluttered.

He wore Ti-Lore clothing as well. Brown trousers made of a tough fabric tucked into shin-high boots, and a black, sleeveless shirt trimmed in fur that showed off his muscular arms.

Now she knew he could do amazing things to her body. Last night had been the best night of her life. As he'd promised, he'd shown her so many wonderful things.

She knew in her bones that this man was hers.

She just needed to prove it to him now.

Azulon was talking with the newcomers and introducing them to Sten. When she got close, Sten held out a hand to her, and she took it.

"Carys, this is Wexor," Sten said. "He's the leader from the neighboring village."

She nodded at the tall Ti-Lore man, whose long hair was in thick braids. He had beaten metal jewelry in his ears. She bowed her head. "Thank you for coming."

"Azulon said you are enemies of the Gek'Dragar." His voice was deep and steady. "That makes us allies." Wexor waved a hand.

Another Ti-Lore warrior stepped forward and set some fabric on the ground. He rolled it out to uncover several metal parts inside.

All in pieces.

Her stomach dropped.

"This is your communicator," Azulon said.

Sten's mouth flattened.

"It doesn't work, I'm afraid." Wexor looked apologetic. "It was damaged when we fled our mountain village."

Sten crouched, and Carys bit her lip. This was no good to them.

Sten picked up some of the parts, studying them. Then he looked up. "I might be able to fix it. Azulon, do you have any tools?"

The man nodded. "Some."

"Okay, if you can—"

A warrior sprinted into the village, sweating and puffing. He said something in a long string of the local language, and sharp gasps echoed all around.

"What's wrong?" Carys asked.

Azulon's face was grim. "Gek'Dragar ships are headed this way."

Her chest locked. *No.*

Sten rose. "They must have tracked us here."

"No," Azulon said. "They do regular visits, to ensure we are not plotting against them." He turned his head and spat on the ground. "Come, and bring the communication unit."

Sten scooped up the fabric and slid an arm around Carys.

"Thank you, Wexor," she said.

The other Ti-Lore nodded. "Be safe."

Azulon led them to another hut. Inside, it looked like a meeting place with a thick, well-worn rug, and lots of chairs. Several Ti-Lore villagers swept aside the furniture and lifted the rug. There was a trap door beneath.

Crouching, Azulon opened it. "I'm sorry. It is dark and cramped, but you will be safe here."

They'd etched a small cellar into the hard ground.

Sten leaped in with the comm parts, then lifted Carys down.

"I will return when they are gone," Azulon said. "Stay still and quiet."

"Be careful," Carys said.

The Ti-Lore leader nodded, then closed the door, concealing them in darkness.

Sten pulled her onto his lap, and she pressed into him.

"If they find us…"

"They won't." He squeezed her hip.

"Can you really get the comm unit working?"

"I don't know, but I'm going to try."

She pressed her face to his neck, breathing in his warm skin. "I'm so glad you're with me. You sacrificed your own freedom when you put that dura-binding on us. You could've been back on Oron, safe—"

"Being with you, protecting you, that's the most important thing in my life."

She kissed him. "I love you, Thorsten."

He drew in a ragged breath, and he started to speak. She pressed her fingers to his lips.

"Don't say anything."

"I'm not and will never be good enough for you." She felt him shake his head. "And I am not a man comfortable with discussing my…feelings. Especially ones I've spent a lifetime denying."

"Last night you were perfect for me." She rubbed against him. "I decide who's right for me, not you."

Muffled noises came from above.

"Shh," he said.

They sat there like statues, hardly daring to breathe, and her pulse pounded wildly. She gripped Sten's wrists, and prayed their new Ti-Lore friends were okay.

It felt like forever, but finally, she heard noises above them, and the trap door opened.

For a horrible second, she wondered if the Gek'-Dragar had found them.

Azulon's serious face looked down. "It is safe." He helped them out.

"Is everyone okay?" she asked.

The man sighed. "It was just the usual threats. They're searching for you." His face darkened. "They offered a large reward of food and goods to turn you in. My people are honorable, but many of the villages have little food, and people are starving. I can't guarantee your safety forever."

"I understand," Carys said. She could hardly blame someone for wanting to feed their family.

Sten looked grim. "I'll get to work on the comm unit."

They moved back to the hut they'd slept in, and Sten spread the components out on the table. Azulon brought him some tools. There was a crease in his brow as he sat down and got to work.

"Knightqueen?"

She dragged her gaze off Sten and looked at Azulon. "Yes?"

"Our scout who warned us of the Gek'Dragar has brought disturbing news."

He looked so serious, and her belly tightened into knots. "What is it?"

"He spied on a group of Gek'Dragar. One was very

important. A commander. They were laughing and talking of their impending victory against the Oronis."

Dread filled her. "Go on."

"We knew that they've been experimenting with the *plorion,* the mining fluid we developed."

Oh, no. "And?"

"They've used it to create a weapon. A terrible weapon."

"What?" Sten barked.

"We questioned a Gek'Dragar we captured," Carys said. "He mentioned a weapon that would consume us."

Azulon nodded. "The scout said they call it the Blue Death. They have altered the *plorion*. My scout wasn't clear on all the details, but he believes they've made an airborne variant." There was deep regret on his face. "And...the first target is Oron."

"No," she breathed. If that mining fluid was made more virulent and airborne, just one breath of it would be lethal.

Her people were at risk. Billions of lives.

"I wish now that my people never created that fluid." Azulon shook his head violently. "It has brought us nothing but heartache."

She touched his hand. "It is not your people's fault. The blame lies with the Gek'Dragar. They twist and destroy everything they touch. I *will* stop them. My knights will stop them, and I promise to help free Ti-Lore as well."

"The Blue Death could destroy your world," the Ti-Lore said.

"My knights and I will never let that happen." She

squeezed his hand. "I formally accept the Ti-Lore as allies of the Oronis. Everything you've done for us will help me defeat the Gek'Dragar."

Azulon bowed his head. "You do me and my people a great honor, Knightqueen."

Sten stood. "I got the comm unit working."

She whirled, and her pulse leapt at the sight of lights blinking on the comm unit.

They could send a message.

STEN WATCHED CARYS PACE. Her movements were jerky, and he hated seeing her upset.

She spun. "Anything?"

"Not yet." He rose and rested his hands on her shoulders. She was so tense. "We only just sent the message ten minutes ago. It could take time to reach any Oronis or our allies."

But they both knew no one might get it. Ti-Lore had to be deep in Gek'Dragar space. He massaged her shoulders. The message was encoded in such a way that only the Oronis could decrypt it.

If the Gek'Dragar intercepted it, it would only be gibberish.

But to get help, it needed to reach their knights.

"We have to be patient."

She made a sound, whirled, and paced across the hut. "How? The Gek'Dragar have a deadly weapon, Sten. That mining fluid ate away at the mountains here and twisted the animals. Now, whatever they've done to make it even more toxic, they're going to unleash it on Oron." Her voice broke.

He hugged her to his chest.

"I have to stop them." She clutched at him.

"You're not alone, Carys. *We'll* stop them, along with your entire Knightforce."

She held on to him, then she leaned up and kissed him.

He hauled her close. He'd never get enough of her.

He knew they needed to escape and stop the Gek'-Dragar, but a part of him didn't want to leave. Here, on Ti-Lore, she was his. He knew that when they left, everything would change.

Once again, she would be the knightqueen.

He boosted her up and she slid her legs around his waist.

"*Sten.*" She cupped his stubbled cheeks.

Emotion welled in his chest. He needed to tell her how he felt. "Carys, I—"

There was a whoosh of sound overhead. He tensed. Another Gek'Dragar patrol?

He heard the Ti-Lore shouting.

Carys wriggled to get down.

"Stay back." He went to the doorway, careful not to be seen.

When he peered through, he sucked in a breath.

"Sten?"

"It's a shuttle."

She gripped his arm. "The Gek'Dragar?"

"No." He met her gaze. "It's Terran."

Her mouth fell open. "Terran?" She shook her head.

KNIGHTQUEEN

"How? The Terrans are new allies and not as technologically advanced. How could they be this far out in Gek'-Dragar space?"

He took her hand. That was something he was keen to find out. They stepped outside.

He watched a pair of Terrans in dark-blue Space Corps uniforms disembark from the silver shuttle. They were watchful, with small blaster weapons in their hands.

Then two tall, very familiar Oronis knights stalked off the shuttle in full black armor, three-quarter length cloaks draping down their backs.

"Knightmaster Nea," Sten said. "Knighthunter Kaden."

Knightmaster Nea Laurier was tall and fit, with bold features, and her black hair in a long braid. Knighthunter Kaden Galath was her opposite, tall and lean, with short, platinum-blond hair and a haughty face with high cheekbones.

When Nea saw them, her face lit up. "Thank the stars." She bowed her head to Carys. "Knightqueen." Then Nea slapped Sten's shoulder. "I'm so very happy to see you both."

"How did you get here?" Carys asked.

"It's a long story." Nea tipped her head at the Terrans. "And we had some help."

"Knightqueen Carys, I'm Chief Engineer Watson," an older woman said. She had a no-nonsense air, a weathered face, and graying brown hair pulled up in a bun. "And this is Ensign Noth."

The young, clean-cut man smiled at them.

Carys smiled back. "Thank you for coming for us."

"Nea and I broke into the Gek'Dragar prison to rescue you." Kaden pulled a face. "You ruined our plan by escaping."

"That was you?" Sten said.

Kaden nodded. "We've been searching for you ever since."

"And dodging the Gek'Dragar," Nea added. "They're searching for you, too. We should leave, Carys."

Carys nodded and turned to Azulon. She took his hands. "Thank you, Azulon. Your help, and the help of your people, has been invaluable. Without you, we might not have survived."

"We are united by our enemy, Knightqueen," the Ti-Lore said. "And now by our friendship."

"I vow to stop the Gek'Dragar. Ti-Lore *will* be free again."

"Thank you." He bowed his head.

"Carys, we should go." Sten pressed a hand to her back. "The Gek'Dragar could detect the Terran shuttle."

She waved to the kids. Malthor was waving madly at them. Beside her son, Nythoria raised a hand in farewell. Sten led Carys onto the shuttle.

The interior was mostly silver, with blue accents. The passenger seats were plush, and the Terrans moved toward the cockpit.

"Strap in, your Highness," the ensign said.

They found seats. Kaden and Nea sat across from them.

"Ashtin sent you after us?" Carys asked.

Nea nodded. "It was a long journey."

Sten knew the pair didn't get along. They'd been rivals since their Academy days.

"A *very* long journey," Nea said. "Into Gek'Dragar space. Lucky for us, the Terrans have a different cloaking technology to ours. One the Gek'Dragar can't detect. It meant we could slip in here undetected."

"We owe a lot to our new allies," Kaden said.

"We do." Nea smiled at him.

Then shockingly, the knighthunter leaned over and kissed Nea.

And Nea kissed him back.

Carys blinked at them.

Sten's brows creased. "You're...together?"

"Yes," Nea said.

"But you...hate each other," Sten said.

"Not anymore," Kaden said with a smile. "In fact, we're married. Captain Attaway married us on the Terran ship."

Sten's eyebrows winged up, shock keeping him silent.

Beside him, Carys laughed. "Congratulations."

"It's a *really* long story." Nea grinned. "And Knightmaster Ashtin fell in love with a Terran."

"Sub-Captain Kennedy Black?" Carys' eyes lit up. "I *knew* he liked her."

"He sure does," Nea said. "She's the new Terran liaison to the Oronis. They're taking care of things on Oron."

Then Carys' smile faded. "It's imperative we get back."

Kaden's brow creased, and he studied her intently. "What's wrong?"

"The Gek'Dragar have developed a weapon," Carys said.

"It's based on a mining fluid the Ti-Lore developed," Sten added.

Kaden cursed. "The one that ate away the rocks and mountains?"

Sten nodded. "The Gek'Dragar overused it. And now, they've apparently engineered it to be even worse and made it airborne."

The two knights shared a worried look.

"They call it the Blue Death," Carys said. "And they plan to unleash it on Oron."

"No," Nea breathed.

"We will *not* let that happen," Carys said fiercely.

"Everyone hold on," the ensign called back. "We're about to leave atmosphere. There are some Gek'Dragar patrol ships in range, so we need to sneak through and get back to the *Helios* as fast as we can."

Carys leaned back in her seat.

Sten wanted to touch her, but curled his fingers into his palms.

He made himself look straight ahead. Now that they were no longer on Ti-Lore, he was once again just her knightguard.

He couldn't let himself forget that.

CHAPTER FOURTEEN

It felt surreal to step onto the Terran ship.

Carys looked around with interest. The vessel was so bright, and spotlessly clean, which was such a contrast to the last week of her life.

Sten was one step behind her, silent and protective, as they entered the bridge of the *Helios*. A large viewscreen dominated the forward wall, and rows of consoles sat in front of it. Most of the consoles had no one sitting at them.

"Knightqueen Carys, I'm Captain Attaway." A uniform-clad woman with short, blonde-brown hair strode forward, hand extended. "We're all so glad you're all right."

"Captain." She took the woman's hand and shook in the way Terrans did. "You have my greatest gratitude for coming after me and Knightguard Sten. Thank you."

"It was the least we could do."

"I know you risked a great deal, and I'm thankful."

"Knightqueen." Nea stepped forward. "You need to go to Medical to get checked."

"I'm fine, really—"

"You'll get checked." Sten's voice brooked no argument.

She shot him a look. "Then you will, too."

His mouth flattened. "As my queen commands."

Her belly clenched, thinking of the last time he'd said that phrase. But now, he looked like a robot, his face impassive. There was no sign of the man who'd loved her so thoroughly.

"We're ready to get underway," the captain said. "Let's set our route to Oron."

The few crew members on the bridge tapped at their consoles.

The ship's engines rumbled, vibrating the floor beneath Carys' feet. She stared at the image of Ti-Lore on the viewscreen. Even from space, she could see the vast mountain ranges that crossed the planet, and dense greenery at the poles.

We will not forget you.

"Come, Carys," Sten said.

She let him lead her off the bridge.

Nea and Ensign Noth led them down some corridors. The knightmaster stopped and pressed her palm to a panel. The door slid open with a quiet hiss. Medical was bright, clean, and well-organized, and empty of staff.

"Your Highness, I'm afraid I'm all there is to run the scanner," the young ensign said. "I'm sorry we don't have a full crew."

"We only took volunteers for a skeleton crew to travel

into Gek'Dragar space," Nea explained. "They've done an excellent job."

"I'm sure you'll do a fine job as a stand-in healer, Ensign." Carys sat up on one of the bunks. The young man moved a scanning unit over her. It beeped.

"You're in good health. It appears your minor wounds are already healing themselves, thanks to your implants." He held up an injector. "I'd like to give you an antibiotic stimulant."

She nodded and he pressed it to the side of her neck.

"Now check Sten," she said.

Her knightguard crossed his muscular arms. "My injuries are healing too—"

"I don't care. You almost died a day ago."

He grunted and sat on the bunk beside hers. He grumpily let the ensign treat him.

"Do you have any more intel on the Gek'Dragar weapon?" Nea asked.

"No." Carys jerked her gaze off Sten. "All we know is that it uses the mining fluid. The Ti-Lore call it *plorion*. And that it will destroy all life on Oron."

Nea's face hardened. "The Gek'Dragar must have it aboard a cloaked ship to transport it. I'll send word to Ashtin to monitor for all incoming ships to Oron."

"Excellent. Thank you, Nea."

"Knightguard Sten, you're also fine," Ensign Noth said. "I see where you had some internal injury but it's healing up just fine."

"I've assigned cabins to both of you." Nea smiled. "I'm guessing you'd like a hot shower, and to get some decent sleep."

Sten nodded. "Thanks, Nea. It's imperative that Carys rests."

Carys frowned at him. He was speaking so coolly. Like they were nothing. Just a queen and her guard.

She hated it. Her hands flexed on the edge of the bunk beneath her.

"Carys?"

Nea's voice made her look up. Everyone was looking at her, so she guessed the knightmaster had asked her something.

"I'm sorry. I'm just tired." She glanced at Sten again, and found his rugged face blank.

"Of course," Nea said. "Food has already been sent to your cabins. Go. Get some sleep. We should be out of Gek'Dragar space soon. The Terran cloaking system is very effective, but still experimental. We burned it out once on the way here. So, if it fails again, I'd prefer to be back in Oronis space."

Carys slid off the bunk. "Thank you, Nea. You risked so much to find us."

The knightmaster bowed her head. "It's my honor and duty." She looked up. "Sten, can I have a moment of your time to debrief?"

"Of course," he replied.

Carys choked back her frustration. She'd wanted to see him. Alone.

And smack him for practically ignoring her.

Had his feelings changed? Did he no longer feel what he felt when they'd been alone on Ti-Lore?

She walked alone down the corridor. He'd never actually said how he felt. She knew that he was attracted to her, but...ugh. She *hated* feeling like this. Uncertain and questioning everything.

She reached her assigned cabin and touched the door control. It opened.

"Welcome Knightqueen Carys," a modulated computer voice said.

The cabin was nice and spacious. There was a tray of food resting on the built-in table and a small, adjoining washroom. Walking over, she picked at some fruit and cheese on the tray, but her stomach was too knotted for her to eat. She headed for the washroom.

Maybe a shower would help? She carefully stripped off the Ti-Lore outfit. She'd have it cleaned and keep it.

The hot shower brought tears to her eyes. It brought back memories of the heated mineral pool. She washed her hair several times, then flicked off the water and stepped into the dryer.

Clean and dry, she felt a little more normal. She found a silky, white robe hanging on a hook and pulled it on. She brushed her hair, then used several of the lotions and moisturizers she found in the drawers.

Now, she needed to hunt Sten down.

She would *not* stand by and let him freeze her out. She nodded at her reflection in the mirror. She'd find him and tell him exactly what she thought.

She'd barely taken two steps into her cabin when the door chimed.

She touched the door controls, and found Sten standing on the other side, showered and changed. His hair was damp, and he smelled of something woody.

"My queen—"

She gripped the front of his shirt and yanked him into the cabin.

"Say my name, Thorsten."

He met her gaze. "Carys."

She put her hands on her hips. "Since we came aboard this ship, you've acted like...like you've never touched me. Or kissed me. I hate it." She threw her hands in the air. "Are you just going to ignore me now?" She poked him in the chest. "Pretend that nothing ever happened between us?"

He stepped forward and yanked her to him, and then his mouth was on hers.

STEN PLUNDERED her mouth until she was breathless.

Not touching Carys in front of the others had almost killed him. He lifted his mouth and watched as she licked her lips.

"That's much better," she whispered.

He nudged her back until she sat on the edge of the bed. He knelt in front of her.

"I am yours. I will always do what is best for you. Out there, you are the knightqueen. That's a fact."

"Sten—"

"But in here, I'm yours in every way. A man who will do everything he can to cherish you."

She released a long breath. "Anything?"

"Yes."

"Then rise."

He stood, towering over her.

"Now strip, my knightguard."

He unfastened his shirt and pulled it off. Her hot gaze ran over him. The raw appreciation left no doubt how much she liked his body.

He kicked his pants off and was naked before her, his cock rising, thick and proud.

"You please me, Sten. Everything about you." She jerked her head. "Sit."

He saw the chair at the built-in desk, unlatched it, and sat.

She rose, all lithe grace. Her robe had loosened, giving him glimpses of her naked body—the curve of her breasts, the slope of her belly. His gut tightened. Her skin was sleek, and she smelled like flowers.

She ran a hand along his shoulders. "I love how broad you are." Her fingers danced across his chest. "I love your strength."

He closed his eyes and felt her press a kiss to his shoulder. He shuddered.

"I love how you react when I touch you. How I affect you."

"You'd affect any man."

She nipped his ear. "You know I don't care about other men. I care about you." She traced the scars on his cheek. "You got these for me. Protecting me."

"I'd die for you."

She stepped in front of him, frowning. "That is something I don't want. I'd prefer for you to live for me."

"As my queen commands."

She straddled him and he grunted. He went to touch

her, but she pushed his hands down to the arms of the chair.

"I'm touching you, Sten." Her lips nibbled his and then she kissed him. He groaned into her mouth. "I want you to enjoy my touch, and when we're outside this cabin, I want you to still feel it. To be imagining the next time I touch you." She undulated, rubbing against his cock teasingly.

"I'm always imagining touching you."

"Good."

He saw her desire, scented it. He got another glimpse of her full breasts through the robe.

"Who do you belong to?" she murmured.

"You, Carys. Always."

She licked her lips, rubbing faster now, and he felt how wet she was. He gritted his teeth. It was pure torture, and his body vibrated with need.

"One day, I will touch you in front of others. Let them see what you mean to me."

He frowned. "Carys...?"

"Shh. No more talking." Her voice was breathy. "Sten?"

"Yes."

"I...want you to touch me now."

"Are you done with your teasing?"

Her hands tightened on his shoulders. "Yes. I want you inside me now. And Sten, make me feel it."

With a growl, he surged up. He tore the robe off her body and turned her. He bent her over the built-in desk.

She gasped, bracing herself. He knew he was being

rough, but she'd pushed him to the edge. He wanted to take her roughly, have her accept him in every way.

He stroked between her thighs. "You like that?"

"*Yes*," she breathed.

He slid a hand into her hair, and pushed his fingers inside her. "You're so wet, Carys."

"For you."

He pressed his body to hers, then moved up to work that tantalizing nub between his fingers. She cried out his name.

"You'll feel this, Carys." He withdrew his hand, and rubbed the head of his cock through her soft folds. "You'll feel my possession. I won't be gentle."

"Good."

Then he surged inside her. With a short scream, she arched her back.

"When we get back to Oron, when you're wearing an elegant dress, standing in front of your people, you'll still feel me between your legs. No one will know, except you and me." He thrust hard. "No one will know that you had your big brute of a guard between your legs."

She moaned.

He thrust harder, rougher. He wanted to claim her in every way.

"Sten?"

His fingers tightened in her hair. "Yes."

"I want to see your face. I want to watch when you come inside me."

His gut clenched so hard it was painful. He pulled out of her, and she moaned. He spun her and lifted her off her feet. He carried her to the bed and set her down.

Then he covered her body with his, settling between her legs.

She smiled at him.

He couldn't talk, he needed to be back inside her.

This time, he filled her slowly. He watched wonder spread over her face.

"You feel so right." She cinched her legs tight against his sides.

Sten rocked into her, drowning them both in the searing pleasure. His gaze locked on hers. "My queen."

"My Sten."

He watched as she came, then he followed her over the edge.

CHAPTER FIFTEEN

Carys stepped off the Terran shuttle and pulled in a deep breath. A warm breeze swirled around her, carrying the scent of *tallia* flowers. The warm sun hit her skin.

She was home.

Her chest squeezed. She realized now that during her captivity, and while she and Sten had been on the run on Ti-Lore, a part of her had wondered if she'd ever see Oron again.

Ahead of her, rows of knights were standing at attention in the castle courtyard. Beyond them was the shining city of Aravena—the capital city of Oron. The purple-tinged waters of the River Camlann wound through the city. Elegant buildings speared into the sky, and graceful arches of bridges crossed the river.

Behind her, the castle's spires, all made of gleaming-white stone and blue glass, shone in the sun, while the lower tiers were filled with greenery and gardens.

Her planet was all shining and beautiful. Her people lived in peace and prosperity.

Unlike those on Ti-Lore. Unlike those on the other planets that the Gek'Dragar had subjugated.

And now her enemy wanted to destroy Oron.

No. It wasn't happening. She wouldn't let it.

She lifted her hand and waved to her knights. Knightmaster Ashtin stepped forward. He stood tall and straight, wearing black pants, a high-necked doublet, and a three-quarter-length cloak. He had a handsome face and black hair. Beside him was a woman in a dark-blue Space Corps uniform that showed off her athletic build. Her brown hair was tied up in a ponytail, and a keen intelligence glimmered in her eyes. Sub-Captain Kennedy Black of Earth. The woman Ashtin had fallen in love with.

The head of Carys' Knightforce stopped in front of her. "Knightqueen." Emotion crossed his face. "Carys, we are so pleased to have you home."

She took his hands and squeezed. "Thank you for everything you've done, Ashtin. To find me and Sten. To keep things running here on Oron."

Sten stepped up beside her, and he and Ashtin clasped hands.

"And I hear congratulations are in order." Carys glanced at Kennedy.

"It's a pleasure to see you again, Knightqueen." The Terran bowed her head.

"I hear you're family now, Kennedy." Carys squeezed the woman's hand. "I despaired that anyone would ever capture the heart of our dedicated knightmaster, here. It seems he was waiting for the right woman from Earth."

Kennedy smiled. "Well, he captured my heart right back, your Highness."

"Please call me Carys. And I'm very happy for the both of you." She shot Sten a quick glance.

"You're both okay?" Ashtin asked, scanning them.

"We're fine. Sten did a very good job of keeping me safe."

Her knightguard grunted.

"The people need to know that you're all right," Ashtin said. "They need to see it with their own eyes. I've scheduled an appearance on the main balcony so that they can see you."

Carys nodded. "Of course. But we have greater concerns, Ashtin. The Gek'Dragar have a weapon."

His face hardened, and Kennedy pressed a hand to his arm.

"Nea and Kaden sent me a report. The Blue Death."

"We *have* to stop the weapon," she said. "And stop the Gek'Dragar once and for all."

"We will," Sten growled.

They were ushered into the palace. As she took in the familiar glossy Camlann marble floors and the high ceilings, pleasure filled her. *Home.* Sten kept pace beside her, once again the stoic knightguard. Her mouth pressed into a line. He was doing his robot impression again, and keeping a distance between them.

She wanted everyone to know they were together. When would the man accept that she loved him? That she wanted *him*, not some handsome prince or diplomat.

"Your Highness." Her maids appeared with a swish of skirts, bobbing curtsies. "We have a gown laid out for you and we can do your hair. For your appearance on the balcony."

Carys nodded. She remembered now how much of her life was dominated by the task of being the knightqueen. She hadn't thought she'd miss Ti-Lore, and the freedom she'd had to shed some of the sometimes tedious trappings of her life.

Then she felt a small touch on her hand. Just a brush. Her head jerked up. Sten wasn't looking at her, but his fingers brushed hers again. Warmth ignited in her chest. She let her small finger curl around his for a second.

"I'll leave you to get ready." He nodded. "I'll come back to get you when it's time."

She desperately wanted to kiss him, but instead, she followed her maids into her quarters. The large room was decorated in her favorite colors of blue and green. Her large, four-poster bed faced the large, curved windows. Several plants sat in ornate pots around the room.

Yes, it was nice to be home.

Her gaze moved straight to the bed. Instantly, she pictured Sten's large, muscular body in it, and she suppressed a shiver.

On the bed lay a beautiful dress. It was white, and would drape her body. It had several long insets of glimmering gold.

Her maids hurried around dressing her. Her hair was piled up on her head, and light makeup dabbed on her face. They tightened the straps so the dress fit her body perfectly, the fabric silky against her skin. It felt strange to be wearing fancy clothes again.

One of the maids came forward, holding a flat, gold box. Carys' crown rested inside. She reached out and stroked it. Her mother had worn it. Carys had so many memories of being a little girl, stroking it in fascination. It was made of delicate black and gold spikes of metal.

She'd been wearing it at the ball when she'd been abducted. She hadn't known what had happened to it.

She lifted the crown and settled it on her head.

There was a brisk knock at the door.

"Enter," she said.

Ashtin and Sten strode in. Her gaze ran over her knightguard. He was wearing his black armor, with a three-quarter cloak draped off his broad shoulders. He was every bit the knightguard.

"Ready?" Ashtin asked. "Crowds have gathered in the streets below the castle. The people have heard you're back."

She nodded. "I'm ready."

The men flanked her. They strode out of her quarters and down the corridor toward the main balcony that faced the city.

As they neared, two knightguards opened the doors for them.

Up this high, she could see all of Aravena. The tall buildings, many of them draped in greenery, the smaller buildings that were homes and small businesses, the tree-filled parks and squares.

Down below, she saw the streets were packed with people. Her throat tightened. They were all waving gold flags. When she stepped up to the railing, and they saw her, cheers broke out. She heard whistles and happy cries.

She pressed a hand to her chest, tears welling in her eyes. She hadn't realized how much her disappearance had affected her people.

I will keep you safe. I will protect you with everything I have.

She waved, turning from side to side. The cheers intensified. She glanced at Sten, and he gave her a small nod.

Then she dropped her hand and stepped back. Her smile dissolved. "Now, we need to discuss the Gek'Dragar."

Ashtin gave her a brisk nod. "To the war room."

Back inside, she took off her crown and handed it to her maid. Her heels clicked on the marble floor as she followed the men down several levels.

Two knights stood at attention at the metal doors leading into the war room. As they approached, the pair pushed the doors open.

Inside was a huge light table with projections streaking up above it. Around it stood Nea, Kaden, Kennedy, and Captain Attaway.

"Have we had any luck locating the Gek'Dragar ship we believe is carrying the weapon?" Carys asked, walking up to the light table.

"Not yet," Nea said. "Everyone is searching for it, and all our ships are on high alert. Captain Attaway's about to leave with the *Helios* to help."

The Terran captain nodded. "Our scanning systems

are different from yours. There might be a chance we can detect something."

"War Commander Davion Thann-Eon has been in touch. There are several Eon warships on the way.

Carys knew their alliance with the Eon warriors was rock-solid. Their advanced warships would be invaluable. "Remind me to thank King Gayel."

"You can do it in person," Ashtin said. "He's en route aboard the *Rengard*."

She pressed a hand to the light table, looking at all the planets and stars that made up Oronis space. Each one of them represented Oronis people who she needed to protect.

"I will *not* let the Gek'Dragar hurt my people." She looked right at Sten. "I will protect everyone I care about."

His gaze stayed steady on hers.

Then she looked at Ashtin. "Do whatever it takes to find that ship."

STEN CHECKED in with his knightguards.

His men and women crowded around him, slapping his arm and back, happy to see that he'd survived.

"What you did for the knightqueen..." one man shook his head, awe on his face. "Putting that dura-binding on was brilliant. You're an inspiration, Knightguard Sten."

"We've heard a little of your ordeal on the alien planet, and what you faced," a female knightguard said. "You protected the queen every step of the way."

Several of them bowed their heads at him, showing their respect.

His chest felt tight. "I did what any knightguard would do. And I had help. Our queen is tough and a fierce fighter."

He'd also bedded the queen. Put his hands on her slim, beautiful body.

Claimed her as his.

What would they think of that?

He cleared his throat. "The Gek'Dragar are coming. For our queen, for all of us. Double patrols around the castle. I want security increased."

"It's true they have a deadly weapon?" another guard asked.

"It is. Everyone must remain on high alert."

His people nodded and leaped into action. Several peppered him with questions. He answered, watching as they hurried off to do their jobs. They were good people. Dedicated and honorable.

"Knightguard Sten?"

A young knightguard, fresh out of the Academy, stood in front of him.

"I just wanted to say it's an honor to serve with a man like you." The man bowed and left.

Sten stared after him. He'd known they were all dedicated to the knightqueen, and to Oronis. He just hadn't realized how dedicated they were to him as well.

His hands balled into fists. They had to stop the Blue Death from reaching Oron. Whatever it took.

He strode to the windows, staring out over the city. Night was starting to fall, and he thought this was the prettiest time in Aravena. When the lights of the buildings all started to glitter. It looked like the night sky reflected on the land.

Ashtin appeared at his side. "How are you doing? It must be a little jarring to be back on Oron after everything you've been through."

Sten nodded. "I'm glad we're back. And that Carys is safe."

"It had to be rough."

"It was. But it's rougher for the people that the Gek'-Dragar have subjugated. They ruined Ti-Lore." He shook his head. "The Gek'Dragar have to be stopped, Ashtin. It's not enough to just win one battle. We need to end this. I won't let them come near Carys again." His tone was low and fierce.

Ashtin stared at him.

Sten scowled. "What?"

"You're in love with her."

Sten froze.

"Having just recently fallen in love myself, I recognize it now. And I suspect you've loved her for a long time."

Sten felt an itchy, uncomfortable feeling wash over him. "She's our queen. I'm her knightguard."

"But she's not just the queen to you."

Sten's jaw tightened. "Ashtin—"

"I think you're good for her. Steady and loyal."

Sten blinked. "What?"

"She lost everything when she was young. She's strong, but everyone needs a solid foundation, something to hold them steady."

Heart pounding, Sten scoffed. "She's elegant and refined. Beautiful and smart. I'm just a battle-hardened guard who grew up on a farm."

"So?"

Sten made an annoyed sound.

"And I was an orphan with no family. It doesn't change my achievements or the man I am."

"But the woman you love isn't the knightqueen of Oron."

Ashtin's gaze narrowed. "So, you're fine with her making an alliance? Marrying some foreign prince or planetary leader?"

Something exploded inside Sten's chest. He whirled, then pressed his forearm to his friend's neck and shoved him against the wall.

Ashtin just smiled. "I thought not."

"She is...everything good and beautiful." Sten stepped back, releasing Ashtin. "In my heart, she's mine." He released a harsh breath. "I'm not king material, Ashtin. Like I said, I'm not polished or diplomatic."

"Does Carys care about any of that?"

"The people will care."

"You're a good man, Sten. Don't worry about the people. All you need to worry about is Carys and how she feels."

"I can't be king."

"A king supports his queen. He cares about the planet. He protects the people." Ashtin cocked his head. "That's exactly you. You already do all of that."

Sten felt like a knot had tied itself in his chest. "I don't have tact or diplomacy."

"No, but Carys does." Ashtin slapped his shoulder. "I think the two of you would be a great pair. You'd complement each other. Stop fighting so hard."

His friend left him standing there, and Sten turned back to the window. He stared out over the city for a long time, his thoughts churning.

Then he turned and headed down the hall. Aimlessly, he took several twists and turns. That's when he realized that he'd headed to Carys' personal quarters.

As he approached the door, he saw two of his best knightguards flanking it. When they saw him, they snapped to attention.

"Knightguard Sten," the female guard said.

"As you were."

"Did you need something, Knightguard?" the older man asked.

Sten looked at Carys' door. "Well—"

The door was wrenched open, and Carys stood there wearing a long, loose dress in a pretty blue. "Oh, you're here, Knightguard Sten. You're late for our briefing." She reached out and gripped his arm. Then she yanked him inside.

She slammed the door closed behind them.

"Carys—"

She leaped on him. He caught her, then her mouth was colliding with his as she wrapped her legs around his waist. Her hungry mouth moved against his, and with a groan, he angled his head and took over.

Her lips parted, and he plunged his tongue into her mouth. He pulled in the taste of her, feeling like everything in his world had just righted itself. She rocked against him, her hands digging into his shoulders.

"I missed you," he murmured against her lips.

"I missed you too." She nipped his bottom lip. "Sten, when all this is over, and we've defeated the Gek'Dragar...we'll talk. About us."

He pulled in a breath. "All right. Do you want an update on the Gek'Dragar?"

She pulled a face. "I know the ship still hasn't been located. We'll know when they do find it. For now..." she pressed harder against him, her fingers skimming into his hair. "I don't want to think about the Gek'Dragar."

"And what does my queen want?"

"She wants you in her bed." The corner of her lips curled in a sensual smile. "You're sleeping here, Sten. I have a very large bed, and I won't lie, I've imagined you in it many times." This time, she bit his lip hard.

He slid his palms more firmly under her ass and carried her to the bed. He laid her on it.

"I've imagined being here with you, too."

On the bed, Carys smiled. Then she whipped her loose dress over her head.

All she wore beneath it was a filmy, nearly transparent nightgown that ended at mid-thigh. His stomach clenched. The fabric clung to her breasts and made him hard in an instant.

She held out a hand to him. "You have too many clothes on, Thorsten."

He started unfastening his shirt. "That can be remedied."

CHAPTER SIXTEEN

The emergency alert blasted through Carys' implant.

All senior knights to the war room. All senior knights to the war room.

She jerked awake. She was held in Sten's arms. For a second, she thought she was back on Ti-Lore. But as he sat up and turned on the bedside light, she realized they were in her room at the castle.

She had a naked Sten in her bed. She almost smiled, but she knew he'd heard the emergency alert as well.

He quickly rose and dressed.

"Do you have more information?" She knew he'd be in contact with Ashtin. She slipped off the bed and hurried to pull on some clothes as well.

"Sensors picked up an anomaly. A cloaked ship was spotted near the Kreora moon."

That was close to Oron. She felt like a fist formed in her chest. She quickly pulled on some black trousers and a white wrap shirt that she tied into place.

Let them come. She and her knights would stop them.

Once they were both dressed, Sten pulled open the doors and strode out. There were two guards outside, and two of Carys' maids, who'd clearly rushed from their beds. Everyone froze, startled gazes falling on Sten.

"We need to get to the war room." Carys waved her maids off. "Please, go back to bed."

The maids eyed Sten, then her, then the two of them smiled. Carys couldn't worry about gossip right now. She half jogged to keep up with Sten as he marched down the corridor.

Moments later, they stepped into the war room.

Ashtin was leaning over the light table, frowning. Kennedy was beside him, tapping on a handheld device, with Nea and Kaden. Another pair stood with them.

"Davion," Carys said. "Eve. I didn't know you'd arrived."

War Commander Davion Thann-Eon and his Terran mate Eve looked up. The brunette woman smiled, but her mate's face was set in serious lines. His sleeveless black outfit showed off his brawny arms.

"We arrived an hour ago," Davion said. "We will not leave you to deal with the Gek'Dragar alone."

"Thank you. I hope your son is well."

Eve smiled. "Kane is healthy, far too mobile for his age, and delights in getting into everything."

"We have more warships on the way," Davion continued. "Gayel ordered several to your secondary fleet at the border. In case the Gek'Dragar try to attack on two fronts."

"You have the gratitude of all the Oronis," Carys said.

KNIGHTQUEEN

The warrior inclined his head. "King Gayel is arriving soon. You have our full support."

She swiveled to face Ashtin. "Do you have more intel on the Gek'Dragar ship? How did it get this close? Where is it now?"

It was Kaden who stepped forward, resting his palms on the light table. "It got this close to Oron because it isn't a Gek'Dragar vessel. It's an Urata ship that they're using."

Carys nodded. The Urata were traders and welcome in Oronis space. One of their ships wouldn't raise any suspicion.

"And it's not a cargo ship," Nea said, her face set in hard lines. "From what the sensors detected, it is a warship. A large one."

Carys sucked in a breath, and beside her Sten cursed.

"It will be filled with Gek'Dragar soldiers," Carys said.

"It doesn't matter how many there are," Ashtin snapped. "We will take them down."

"It would be best to take this ship out before it lands on Oron," Kennedy said.

Carys nodded. "Agreed. Do we know its current location?"

"No," Ashtin said. "It's cloaked. We have ships scanning the area, so they can't hide for long."

Sten crossed his arms, staring hard at the map on the light table. She wanted to reach out and touch him.

Then Kaden spoke. "I talked with some of the other knighthunters. Everyone has been reaching out to their networks."

Knighthunters were the Oronis' best spies. She was well aware they had vast networks of contacts across the quadrant and beyond.

"There are whispers that the entire Gek'Dragar leadership is aboard. They want to destroy Oron, and be here to watch it and claim victory. Cement their own greatness." Kaden's lip curled in disgust.

Carys clutched her hands together. "The entire group of eight?" They knew that there were eight Gek'Dragar leaders who sat on the Council. They were the strongest and meanest of all. The stories her knighthunters had gathered said the council were selected by fights to the death.

She straightened. "They think we're weak because we live in peace and harmony. Because we value art, and learning, and beauty. Because we value duty and honor. Because we care for our sick and weak." She whirled, making eye contact with all her people. "We will show them just how strong we are."

Kaden nodded. Nea smiled. The others all met her gaze, steady and composed.

"What makes us strong are our values, our friendships, our family." She looked at Sten. "And our love for one another."

Suddenly, an alarm started blaring, and the lights changed, washing the room in a deep red glow.

"The ship's been sighted." Ashtin leaned forward, swiping the light table screen. "*Gul*. It's approaching Oron in minutes."

Everyone scrambled. Davion made contact with the Eon ships in orbit. Ashtin barked orders to his Knightforce ships. Kennedy tapped on the table, and a projection speared into the air.

Carys saw the huge silver orb of one of Oron's moons. And the outline of a large Urata warship.

"We need the *BlackBlade* to intercept," Ashtin said sharply.

On the screen, the lead Oronis warship swung into view. It was made of pure black metal, and covered in spikes. The forked bow of the ship had a blue ball of energy crackling in the center of it.

Usually, Ashtin would be on the bridge. She could tell from the look on her knightmaster's face that he wished he was there now.

"Stop that ship," he ordered. Then he slammed his hand on the light table. "I should be there."

Kaden stepped up beside Ashtin and gripped his arm. "Come on, then. You'll be better use up there." There was a flash of red light and the men teleported out.

For a second, Carys marveled at Kaden's unique ability. It was very rare among the Oronis.

Kennedy tapped on the table. "Pulling up feed from the *BlackBlade*." Another screen appeared on the table, showing the bridge of the Oronis warship. Kennedy made a sound. "Scans show that the Urata ship is heavily armed."

Suddenly, there was a burst of light, and a sleek Eon warship appeared, coming out of star speed. The front was rounded, but the back tapered in to where the engines sat. It looked like a predator, ready to attack.

"*BlackBlade*, this is the *Rengard*," a deep voice said

across the comm line. "Thought you might like a little help."

"That's War Commander Malax Dann-Jad," Davion said, a smile crossing his face.

Carys watched the *BlackBlade* and the *Rengard* move into formation together. They converged on the Gek'Dragar's Urata ship.

"Urata vessel, I am Knightmaster Ashtin Caydor of Oron. Shut off your engines and stand down. This is your only warning. We *will* open fire."

For a beat, nothing happened.

"The Urata ship is spooling up its weapons!" Kennedy cried.

Then laser fire lit up the screen.

Carys gripped the side of the light table, leaning forward. She heard Ashtin barking orders to his crew. The Urata ship kept firing.

And the *BlackBlade* and the *Rengard* returned it.

She reached out and grabbed Sten's hand. His fingers closed over hers.

Come on. She watched the Urata ship take a direct hit from the *BlackBlade*. *Surrender, you* gul-*vexed bottom feeders.*

The *Rengard's* missiles hit the Urata vessel. It started to list.

"They've lost power," Kennedy said.

Cheers broke out around the room.

Then Carys saw the boxy nose of the vessel tilt toward Oron. Her chest hitched. It had been caught by the planet's gravity.

"*Gul*," Sten said.

The ship, and the Gek'Dragar inside it, were crashing toward Oron.

STEN STRODE down the castle corridor. He was in full armor, his thoughts focused.

A unit of knights marched with him.

"The Gek'Dragar ship crashed outside Aravena on the Lantonas plains," he said. Thankfully, it was mostly farmland out there, and no one had been hurt when the vessel had impacted.

He was sure that the *gul*-vexed Gek'Dragar had been aiming for Aravena.

He stepped outside of the castle and into the morning sunlight. Several rugged vehicles sat waiting for them. They were made of silver-gray metal, with six large wheels. Carys stood in her armor, standing beside Ashtin, Kennedy, Kaden, and Nea.

When she saw him, she nodded. "Let's roll out."

"Everyone to your vehicles," Sten barked.

Knights burst into action. He ducked into the lead vehicle and sat beside Carys. A second later, the vehicle rolled out.

"The plan is to surround the crash site," he said.

They were all hoping that the Gek'Dragar had died in the crash. And that the knights could locate and contain the Blue Death weapon.

"If there are survivors," Carys said. "They will try to unleash the Blue Death."

"And we'll stop them," he said resolutely.

She touched his hand. "We will."

They left the city, moving from the wide roads to the Lantonas plains. It was mostly flat, lush farmland. In areas, crops of yellow and purple flowers grew.

Sten peered through the front screen of the vehicle. Ahead, he saw the twisted wreckage of the Urata ship, smoke rising into the blue sky.

His gut hardened. He saw movement. Gek'Dragar troops were amassing outside the ship.

He activated his comm line. "Ashtin, we're going in hot."

"Good." The other knight's voice came over the line. "Let's do this."

Ashtin sounded ready for a fight.

Sten turned to Carys. Her gaze was narrowed on the crashed ship. He knew she would fight. She was the knightqueen. However much he wished he could lock her away and keep her safe, she would never allow that.

"I'll stay at your side," he said.

She nodded. "I know you will. Let's defend our planet, Thorsten. And destroy the Gek'Dragar leadership once and for all. Their reign of terror is over."

The Oronis vehicles drew closer to the crashed ship.

They pulled up, all the knights exiting and moving into their combat groups. There were several Terrans and Eon warriors to bolster their ranks.

Ahead, several Gek'Dragar soldiers started marching to meet them. They held heavy blasters in their hands.

Sten walked down the line issuing orders. He saw his own group of knightguards and nodded at them. They all nodded back, ready to fight.

"Today, we protect our freedom," Sten said. "Today, we prove our honor. Today, we defend all the innocent people of this planet. We do this with our allies at our sides." He nodded at the Eon, then at the Terrans. "We fight to stop the tyranny of the Gek'Dragar. For honor and duty!"

"For honor and duty!" the Oronis knights bellowed back at him.

He turned, moving back to where Carys was watching him with a small smile. Then she turned to the Gek'Dragar.

"Look," she said.

He saw they were going through the var. Even from a distance, he saw their gray-skinned bodies morphing and bulging.

He ground his teeth together. "*Charge.*"

The Oronis knights started running, their black cloaks whipping out behind them as they picked up speed. He saw blue energy balls being created all across the field. Several of the knights leaped into the air, swords forming in their hands.

Sten had never been prouder to be an Oronis knight.

He ran. Beside him, Carys pumped her slim arms, her glowing blue sword in her hand.

The front knights reached the enemy, and the Gek'-Dragar shouted.

The fight had begun.

A Gek'Dragar soldier appeared in front of Sten, thick tail whipping behind him. Sten slashed and sliced with his sword. He ducked the Gek'Dragar's axe, and thrust his sword through his opponent's middle. He kept going, staying close to Carys as she engaged the enemy.

All around him, knights threw energy balls. Swords whirled and slashed. He spotted Nea, who held a wicked bow in her hands, firing off glowing energy bolts in quick succession. He saw one bolt hit a Gek'Dragar in the eye, sending the alien flying backward.

A Gek'Dragar charged at Sten, holding a combat sword. Sten batted it aside, then launched his own strikes: slash, slice, left, right.

The soldier fell and Sten stepped over him.

Off to the left was a blink of red light. Kaden teleported in right behind another Gek'Dragar, and ran the soldier through with his curved, red sword.

Ashtin leaped into the air, whirling, two balls of energy sparking on each of his hands. He threw them and they smashed into a group of enemy soldiers.

Nearby Kennedy crouched, holding her blaster up, aiming as she fired on the enemy. Sten heard a roar, and turned. Davion, dressed in the signature black-scale armor of the Eon warriors, held a huge sword that also glowed blue. He charged into combat, swinging his weapon with power and skill. Nearby, Eve—wearing matching armor to her mate—swung two smaller swords, no less deadly.

Sten focused on fighting, and assessing any opponent who got too close to Carys.

They battled closer to the wreckage of the ship. More and more Gek'Dragar fell.

Finally, cheers went up.

The lead knights had reached the ship.

Carys stalked through her knights. Sten stayed one step behind her. Some knighthunters had several Gek'-Dragar down on their knees, under guard.

"Where is the weapon?" she demanded.

Ashtin and several other knights moved onto the ship. "We'll search it and look for any remaining Gek'Dragar."

One of the Gek'Dragar prisoners looked up, his teeth covered in blood. "You won't find the weapon." He let out a phlegmy laugh.

Sten stalked over and pressed the tip of his sword to the alien's throat. "Your leaders are dead. Your battle is over. You've lost."

"It will be over when the Oronis dissolve to dust." The Gek'Dragar laughed again. "Our best have taken the Blue Death to your precious capital. We were just the distraction."

Sten rammed the sword forward. The soldier choked, blood streaming down his chest. He sagged forward.

"Knightqueen." Ashtin ran out of the ship, his face in harsh lines "There are signs that a four-man team left the ship."

Sten cursed.

Carys stepped forward. "I will stop them. Sten, Ashtin, Kaden, and Nea, with me. We need to track them and move fast." She turned and looked at Kennedy, Davion, and Eve. "Can I leave you here to coordinate with the knights and secure the starship crash site?"

"Of course," Kennedy said. She looked at Ashtin. "Be careful."

The knightmaster strode to her and gave her a quick, hard kiss.

Carys looked toward the edge of the plains. She studied the ground ahead. It was rockier, covered in trees. It would make it easier for the Gek'Dragar to evade them.

You can't hide for long.

Carys' hand tightened on her sword. "Let's move."

CHAPTER SEVENTEEN

They spread out, running through the trees.

The deep, large prints of the Gek'Dragar were heading in the direction of the city.

Carys kept running. She had to stop them. She couldn't let them unleash the Blue Death.

She drew in a deep breath, and let calmness wash over her. She was resolute.

As the knightqueen, she would protect her people.

"This way," Ashtin called.

She saw her knightmaster turn sharply right, following the tracks on the ground.

They carried on and the trees got thicker. Most had dark-green foliage, but some had needle-like purple leaves.

Then, they broke out of the trees. They stood on the edge of a large clearing. Ahead was a rocky outcrop. She saw the Gek'Dragar at the top, hiding among the boulders.

One big soldier popped up, aiming a weapon at them.

"Watch out!" Ashtin yelled.

Laser fire hit the ground nearby, and Carys rolled. As she got back to her feet, she saw Kaden and Nea duck back into the trees. Then a heavy weight hit her, knocking her off her feet.

Sten pinned her to the ground, covering her body with his. A second later, Kaden and Nea charged out of the trees, one blasting blue energy balls and the other throwing jagged red energy spikes.

"Up, Sten." Carys elbowed him. "They need our help."

He rolled off and helped her up.

"Stop!" a Gek'Dragar yelled from the rocks. "Or we'll release the weapon."

"It's too far from the city," Sten said. "It would dissipate and have little effect."

"They're stalling for time," Ashtin said.

Kaden nodded. "Nea and I will sneak in from behind."

"Go," Carys said with a nod.

As the two knights pulled back, then teleported away, she turned to Sten and Ashtin. "Let's keep the Gek'-Dragar focused on us, so they don't spot Kaden and Nea coming."

Sten smiled. "It'll be my pleasure."

She turned, letting her energy coil inside her. Blue light flared on her palms. Ashtin stepped up on her left, his glowing blue sword in his hand. Sten moved to her right, his broadsword forming.

"Go," she said.

They ran. Carys threw her energy balls, and kept up

a steady rain of them. The Gek'Dragar got off a few shots, but they went wild.

Sten and Ashtin leaped into the air, jumping to the top of the outcrop.

Carys paused at the bottom, throwing more energy at a Gek'Dragar. She saw both knights swinging their swords.

Boom.

The top of the outcrop exploded in a ball of flames.

Carys was lifted off her feet, tossed into the air. She hit the ground and rolled.

Her ears were ringing. *Stars*. Her thudding heart echoed in her ears. *Gul*, had they released the Blue Death?

She scrambled to her feet. Suddenly, Nea was there, pulling her up.

"Are you all right, Carys?"

"The Blue Death?"

Nea shook her head. "Just a regular explosive. It was a trap."

Carys' body locked. "Sten?" She took off at a run.

"Carys!" Nea ran with her.

Sten. If she lost him...

No.

There were rocks and debris everywhere. She scrambled through it. She'd lost her parents, and it had almost destroyed her. She couldn't lose Sten as well.

She climbed up and over the rocks.

She saw Kaden first, the sunlight glinting off the knighthunter's blond hair. Then he shifted.

And she saw Ashtin. He was standing there, bent

over, his hands pressed to his thighs. His head was bleeding.

"Sten?" Her voice was a harsh whisper. She was barely conscious of Nea standing behind her.

Ashtin looked up, his face smeared with soot and blood. "He's okay. Kaden teleported us out...just in time. But Sten hit his head." Ashtin gestured.

That's when she saw Sten lying on the ground, unconscious and still.

Her heart squeezed. She raced over and dropped to her knees beside him. He had soot and dirt on his face. She pressed her hands to his chest. It wasn't until she felt the reassuring rise and fall of that broad chest, and the steady thud of his heart, that she let out a shaky breath.

She leaned down and pressed her lips to his.

When she looked up, her three knights were looking anywhere but at her.

"Do any of you have anything to say?" she said.

"I do," Kaden said.

Nea smacked his arm.

He shot his wife a look, then turned back to Carys. "It's not about you and Sten. He can be obstinate at times, but you'd have to work hard to find a better man."

"Thank you."

"That wasn't what I wanted to say. The Blue Death isn't here, Carys. It looks like one Gek'Dragar escaped."

Her hands clenched on Sten. She wanted to stay with him until he woke, but she had to save her planet.

She touched his face. "I love you."

Then she rose. All her emotions, everything she felt for Sten, her planet and her people, whirled inside her.

All the suffering she'd seen on Ti-Lore. Everything she'd endured at the hands of the Gek'Dragar, it all fused inside her.

She reached deep, thinking about everything they'd taken from her. Her parents. Her childhood. They'd tried to kill her.

Energy pulsed inside her. It was like she could feel the heart of the planet, the heart of her people. She closed her eyes and let it build.

"Carys?" Ashtin's tone was cautious.

She opened her eyes and heard her knights gasp. She realized that her skin was glowing gold, and her hair whipped around her face. It was glowing as well.

"Carys, your eyes are shimmering gold," Nea said.

Energy crackled on Carys' fingertips. It was a gold-tinged blue.

"Take care of Sten. I'll stop the Gek'Dragar and the Blue Death."

STEN GROANED AS HE WOKE, his head throbbing. *"Carys."*

"Take it easy, Sten." Ashtin's voice.

He blinked, pushing through the pain in his head. His chest ached as well, like he'd been stabbed with hot metal. As he sat up, the world swam.

Ashtin, Nea, and Kaden were crouched in front of him, their faces grim.

"You're hurt," Kaden said. "Took a hard knock to the head, and probably have a few broken ribs."

Sten didn't care. He pushed to his feet. *Gul*, it was hard work to get upright. "Where's Carys?"

"A lone Gek'Dragar got away with the Blue Death," Nea said. "She's gone to stop him."

"And you let her go alone?" Sten tried to steady himself, and when he swayed, he bit out a curse.

Ashtin grabbed his arm. "She gave us no choice." His tone was grumpy. "She locked us in with an energy field."

Sten blinked. He turned his head and saw a shimmer of gold around them. He reached out and touched it. It sizzled under his fingers.

"She was...different," Ashtin said.

"She was pulling extra energy from somewhere," Nea said. "She was glowing gold."

Kaden nodded. "She was supercharged."

"I don't care if she has more power. She's not doing this alone." Sten couldn't lose her. He loved her. And being the idiot he was, he still hadn't told her.

He turned to face the energy field. "Help me break this. The four of us should be able to do it."

All four of them pressed their hands to the energy field. Sten pushed all his frustration and fear into it, energy pouring out of him. The others added their energy, and he felt it crackle through the air, raising the hairs on the back of his neck.

A second later, the shield shattered. He watched as it dissipated.

Sten took off at a jog, racing into the trees. He heard the others following behind him.

It wasn't long before he saw Carys' delicate footprints. And nearby, the larger ones of the Gek'Dragar.

A wave of dizziness washed over him. He knew he was hurt, but he locked it down. He *had* to get to Carys. He *would* get to Carys.

The trees grew thicker. He smelled *gnarron* bark and rotting vegetation. Then he raced out of the trees and stumbled to a halt.

They were on a cliff high above the River Camlann. Across the river was Aravena. In the distance, the castle gleamed under the sunlight.

Sten swiveled. *Where was Carys?*

"Why did the Gek'Dragar come this way?" Kaden mused. "If he'd travelled east, he'd have a more direct route to the city."

Sten scanned along the purple waters of the river down below. That's when his gaze fell on a pumping station. There was a narrow, rocky path leading down to the white buildings perched on the water's edge. Water passed through the station to be purified. He froze. "The Blue Death isn't airborne."

"What?" Ashtin said.

"The Blue Death. The Ti-Lore weren't sure what the Gek'Dragar had done to it, they just suspected they'd made it airborne. But that wasn't it, they engineered it for *water*."

Ashtin frowned, then his gaze turned to the river. "*Gul.*"

"The Gek'Dragar wants to put the Blue Death in the river." Which was the main water source for the entire capital city. "It will flow into the city, destroy Aravena, and all the planet's leaders. Then it will keep flowing to the ocean and beyond."

"Then the rest of the planet would be easy to conquer," Nea said quietly.

Without another word, Sten whirled and headed for the path leading down to the pumping station at the water's edge.

Hold on, Carys. I'm coming.

CHAPTER EIGHTEEN

Carys cautiously entered the pumping station.

She heard the rumble of the pumps and the whoosh of water nearby. She moved quietly, making sure her boots didn't make a sound on the stone walkway.

She heard a grunt ahead and let the energy form on her hand. It was wilder than usual, blue and gold spinning together. Power coursed through her veins.

Pressing her back against a wall, she peered around a corner. She spotted the Gek'Dragar's huge form. He held some sort of large glass orb in one of his clawed hands. Inside the orb, a jagged cloud of blue roiled like it was alive.

Like it wanted to get out.

He was approaching one of the pumping station intakes. Purple-tinged water cascaded down a wall and into the river.

As she'd tracked him down here, she'd realized that the Blue Death was meant for the water. He was trying to kill her people by infecting the water supply.

She couldn't let him get that orb into the water.

She stepped out, letting the energy ball on her palm grow. She couldn't toss it directly at him. The risk of hitting the Blue Death was too high.

Instead, she tossed it off to his side.

It hit the floor, sizzling and crackling. The Gek'Dragar dived behind some pumping gear. A moment later, he popped up and fired a laser weapon.

Carys ducked back around the wall.

"You're too late," the Gek'Dragar called out. "This will poison your water and kill your people."

She darted out and slid in behind a pump. She felt the vibrations coming off it. "I won't let you do that. This is my planet and my people. I will stop you."

"The knightqueen herself." He rose, his powerful body flexing. He smiled, showing off his sharp teeth. "This is perfect. My name is Trager. I'm one of the leaders of the mighty Gek'Dragar. I will kill you and your city. Your planet will follow when my fleet arrives."

She rose as well, glaring at him, and snorted. "My ships, along with those belonging to the Eon, are waiting at the border. They will decimate your fleet."

Trager's scaled face stayed impassive, but his tail waved behind him, betraying his agitation.

"Maybe we'll take some losses, but you'll be dead." He spun the orb, the blue fluid inside contracting and pulsing. "And Oron will die."

She shook her head. "The days of the Gek'Dragar destroying planets and innocent people is over." She summoned her energy, everything she could. It rushed to her, rich and pure.

Gold energy crackled over her body. The Gek'Dragar jerked, his eyes widening as he stared at her, some of the confidence leaking from his face.

She thought of Sten. Of the quiet moments and gentle touches, and the way he looked at her with desire in his eyes.

She wanted more time with him.

A lifetime.

But she had to do everything she could to stop this Gek'Dragar.

It was her duty and honor as the knightqueen.

Power swelled inside her and she linked to a deep well that she'd never known existed. For a shining second, she felt like she could feel her mother and father standing at her side.

She'd read the legends of old about the royal bloodlines. The knightkings and knightqueens who'd accessed a higher power to protect the Oronis. A power that shone gold and was more powerful than anything.

The Gek'Dragar spun, sprinting for the water sluice. He held the orb up, ready to throw it.

"No!" Carys leaped forward. Gold energy shot from her hands and snapped out, forming a barrier between the Gek'Dragar and the water.

He threw the orb, but it hit the energy shield and bounced off it.

Carys quickly threw a ribbon of energy into the air and caught the orb. It hovered for a second, then she lowered it to the floor.

Trager let out an enraged screech. He swiveled, green

eyes locking on her as he pulled a combat sword off his back.

Her gold sword formed in her hand. Gold lightning crackled along its blade.

"You will die here." Her voice echoed through the pumping station. "Your plan will fail here."

"No," he hissed.

"You have failed." She advanced. "The Gek'Dragar will be driven back. And I will ensure that you never hurt anyone again."

He leaped at her, and Carys spun to meet him.

Their swords clashed. Her blade cut through his like it was made of fabric.

He stumbled back, shock on his face. He tossed the hilt to the ground and lifted his claws.

She launched a whirlwind of strikes. He tried to dodge, but her blade caught him several times. Deep slashes scored his armor across his chest. He heaved in air.

With a roar, he launched up and grabbed her arms. He spun and tossed her against the wall.

Carys hit, pain reverberating through her body, but a second later, it was gone. The rich energy flowing through her washed it away.

She rose. Trager scrambled across the floor, trying to snatch up the orb.

No. She ran and leaped.

For the Oronis. For Sten.

The Gek'Dragar spun. She saw his eyes go wide. He lifted the orb and threw it at her.

In a split second, she knew she couldn't dodge.

Suddenly, a large form leaped in from the side. The body jumped between her and the orb.

No, Sten. Her heart swelled, rapping against her ribs.

The orb hit him, cracking open. The Blue Death washed over him like a cloud of angry ants. It absorbed into his body, and he dropped to the ground.

With a cry of outrage, Carys let energy spikes form in her hand. She tossed them at the Gek'Dragar. The three sharp, gold blades pierced Trager's chest, pinning him to the wall. He died in an instant.

Carys raced to Sten.

She saw the blue running over him. His armor had crumbled and the veins under his skin bulged, turning bright blue. The bronze color had leached from his skin, turning a pale blue like ice.

"Sten!"

He turned his head toward her, and she saw that his green eyes were now bright blue.

"No! Sten, no."

THE PAIN WAS like icy fingers stabbing into his insides.

Sten tried to breathe, but it was like he had a heavy weight on his chest.

"Sten." Carys dropped to her knees beside him, her face distraught.

"Don't touch him," Ashtin warned. "He's infected."

"Why did you do that?" she breathed. "Why?"

When he'd seen that Gek'Dragar throw the Blue

Death at her, Sten hadn't hesitated. He'd always known he'd give his life for her.

"Save...you. Always." *Gul*, everything hurt.

Tears welled in her beautiful gold eyes. "You cannot die!"

"Carys...you're my reason for being." He dragged in a shuddering breath and realized he couldn't feel his hands and feet anymore. "I love you."

Her lips parted.

"Should've...told you a long time ago."

"I love you too, Thorsten Carahan." She reached out like she wanted to touch him, then her fingers curled into her palms. She looked up at the others. "Get the knighthealers here. Now!"

But Sten knew there was nothing the knighthealers could do. He could feel the Blue Death working through his body. The healers didn't have an antidote for it.

He gasped in air. It was working deep into his cells. Disintegrating his insides.

"I can't lose you." Her voice cracked. "You're my heart. My soul."

"I am...Knightguard Thorsten Carahan. It is my duty to protect...my queen." He wheezed. "I am her sword, her shield, and her devoted servant."

She sobbed. "And I am Knightqueen Carys, the woman who loves you. My loyal guard. My protective lover. *Mine*." Then her jaw tightened, and she shook her head violently. "I won't lose you. I won't lose anyone else I love."

She leaned forward and pressed her hands to his chest.

He heard the others shouting.

"No, Carys!" Ashtin gripped her shoulder. "You'll be infected."

She shrugged him off, then lifted a palm. A wave of energy pushed Ashtin, and he fell back into Kaden.

Sten watched as energy swirled around Carys, sparkling a brilliant gold. Her skin glowed gold, and he heard exclamations from the others.

His mouth dropped open. She was stunning. *Beautiful*. "Carys..."

The gold energy poured out of her and ran over him. It hit him hard, and his back bowed.

It coursed through him, and he gritted his teeth against the powerful sensations.

Then he felt his body lifting off the ground. He opened his eyes and saw Carys was rising off the ground as well. Her hands entwined with his.

The gold wound around them, like ropes. The energy was warm, and it poured into him, washing away the frigid cold.

"Carys." He could breathe again. He wrapped his arms around her as they hovered above the ground. "My love."

Then he kissed her.

She gripped him hard and kissed him back. She molded herself to him, stealing his breath, making his heart beat faster.

He kept kissing her. It took him a while to realize that the gold energy had dimmed, and their feet touched the ground.

He looked down and saw his skin had returned to its

usual bronze color. Then he looked at Carys. The gold glow on her skin was fading.

"You're all right?" Her voice was tight, her face filled with hope.

"Yes," he said. "Thanks to you."

"Good." Then her eyes closed, and she collapsed.

Sten caught her in his arms and lifted her. "We need the knighthealers."

"We'd already called them," Ashtin said. "They're arriving now."

Sten saw three knighthealers making their way down the path to the pumping station. They were led by Knighthealer Taera. The female knight rushed toward them, her eyes locked on Carys.

"Set her down," Taera ordered.

Taera served aboard the *BlackBlade*, and was one of the very best healers. Her implants were geared toward healing.

Sten laid Carys on the ground, but he was reluctant to let her go. He stroked her hair. *Please be okay, sweetness. Please.*

The knighthealer pressed her palm to Carys' chest, energy swelling in the air. She moved her hand over the queen's body, then sat back.

"She's fine. Her vitals are all normal. After some rest, she'll wake."

Sten sagged, his hand clenching in Carys' hair.

Then the knighthealer's gaze switched to Sten. "Now you, Knightguard. I'm told you were exposed to a deadly alien chemical weapon."

"I'm fine."

Taera smiled sweetly. "I don't care."

She lifted her hand, energy pulsing off it.

He glanced at Ashtin. His friend just crossed his arms. "If Carys was awake, she'd order you to get checked."

Sten sighed and nodded.

Taera pressed her hand to his sternum, and he felt a warm glow of energy.

"It appears you're a lucky man, Sten. Whatever the chemical was, it's been neutralized. I detect no sign of it in your body."

"The Blue Death is gone," Nea said, leaning into Kaden.

"Oron is safe," Ashtin breathed.

Emotion shuddered through Sten. "Thanks to our queen."

He lifted Carys into his arms and held her tight.

Something he wanted to do the rest of their lives.

CHAPTER NINETEEN

Carys woke in her bed. The curtains were fluttering in the breeze, and she saw a vase of *verlorna* lilies resting on the table nearby. Their fragrant scent tickled her nose.

She sat up and blinked.

For a horrible second, she thought everything had been a dream: her abduction, the Gek'Dragar and the Blue Death, Sten.

Her heart squeezed.

Sten. He'd been hit with the Blue Death. Horrible images ran through her head. His veins and skin turning blue.

"Carys, you're awake." Nea leaned forward in a chair beside the bed. "Take it easy." The knightmaster held out a glass of water.

Carys ignored the water and gripped the woman's arm. "Sten? Is he all right?"

"He's fine. You and your supercharged energy healed

him." Nea shook her head. "I've never seen anything like it, and Kaden can do some weird things."

"I think it's the power of the royal bloodline."

"Makes sense. Anyway, Ashtin and Kaden bullied Sten into seeing the knighthealers when we got back to the castle. So they could thoroughly check him out. He was still grumbling about it when I left." She smiled. "He asked me to sit with you."

Releasing a breath, Carys dropped back on the pillows. "Thank the knights that he's okay."

Nea's lips twitched. "And thank the knights that the Blue Death was neutralized, and our planet is safe from the Gek'Dragar."

Carys felt heat in her cheeks. "I'm very glad about all of that too."

"The Gek'Dragar fleet tried to come across the border. Our ships, and the Eon warships intercepted them. The last report was that they'd been destroyed, and the few survivors had been driven back. More allies are sending ships. They're going to help the Knightforce free all the planets the Gek'Dragar enslaved."

Carys' chest swelled. "I knew we could do it." She thought of Azulon, Malthor and the others on Ti-Lore. Soon, they'd be free.

But right now, she was tired of being the knightqueen. All she wanted was her knightguard.

"I need to see Sten." She swung her legs over the edge of the bed. She was wearing a robe and she cinched it tightly.

"You fell in love with your knightguard."

Carys looked up at Nea, unable to read the woman's tone. "I fell in love with a loyal, noble man—"

The knightmaster held up a hand. "I'm well aware of all of Sten's good traits." She paused. "Maybe not *all* of them. I know he keeps a lot hidden under his stoic façade, but he's a good man. And personally, I think he'd make an excellent king."

Carys' pulse skipped, then she pulled a face. "So do I, but he doesn't believe that." A cold shiver washed through her. "How can I ask him to do something that he doesn't want?"

"He wants you. He risked his life for you. I think he just hadn't ever pictured himself as a king. He just needs time to adjust, and you need to help convince him. He'd do anything for you."

Yes, he would. "Take me to the knighthealers."

Nea took her arm and helped her out of her room. The palace workers all bowed and called out excited hellos. A few glanced at her bare feet and robe, but didn't comment. She felt a happiness in the air.

As they reached the knighthealers' wing, she could hear Sten complaining from down the hall.

"No more tests. The last ones were all negative. I'm *not* infected and my heart is still beating just fine."

Carys stepped into the airy room. When the knighthealers saw her, they all bowed their heads. Sten sat on one of the wide beds, his arms crossed over his bare chest. He had two sensors stuck to his temples, and another two on his chest.

When he saw her, his arms dropped.

She strode to his bed.

"Carys. Are you—?"

She didn't stop. She climbed onto the bed and into his arms.

She wrapped her arms around him, and his brawny ones closed around her body. She kissed him. Right in front of everyone.

He was stiff at first, and when she pulled back, she saw he was looking at the people behind her.

"You told me you loved me, Thorsten. Was that true?"

"Yes." His voice was gruff. "You know I love you. I've loved you for years, even when I wouldn't admit it to myself. And I'll love you for as long as I have breath in my body."

"And I'll shout my love for you from the rooftops, for everyone to hear. *You* are the right man for me. And for Oron. Look around."

She watched him as he scanned the room. Everyone was smiling at them.

His hands clenched on her hips.

"Be mine," she murmured.

"I am. I always will be."

She swallowed. "Be my king?"

He cupped her cheeks. "As my queen commands."

One week later

STEN LOOKED in the mirror and fiddled with his suit. He tugged at the neckline of his doublet. He hated wearing formal gear.

And he hated balls.

This one would be even worse because he'd be the focus of everyone's attention. It was being held to celebrate his and Carys' betrothal.

Gul, soon he'd become the King of Oron.

The thought left him a little queasy.

But it also meant that Carys would be his wife. The queasiness eased. It would be worth it. He'd walk through fire, and across alien planets, and battle the Gek'Dragar a thousand times to be with her.

Surprisingly, his knightguards had all been thrilled at the news that he was becoming the knightking. They'd even thrown him an impromptu celebration.

He realized now he had their respect and loyalty. Both Ashtin and Kaden had told him that there was no one else who'd make a better king for the Oronis. Because he'd always put the people first.

And he'd always put their knightqueen first.

He left his quarters and strode down the hall, his boots thudding on the marble floor. As he passed people, they bowed their heads to him.

Okay, that would take a little getting used to. He tried not to scowl.

He reached the Grand Hall.

The hall had black stone walls that shone in the light, and were shot through with veins of white and gold. The high ceiling soared overhead. It was covered in an elaborate web that was laden with white vines covered in gold flowers.

The hall was already filled with guests. Thankfully, he spotted Ashtin and Kaden. Both men were wearing similar outfits to his.

They both exaggeratedly bowed their heads at him.

"Your Highness," Kaden drawled.

"Knock it off," Sten growled.

His friends grinned at him. He knew they were teasing, but he still didn't like it. And it was going to take a *really* long time to get used to anyone calling him Your Highness.

"Is Carys here yet?" He scanned the hall but didn't see any sign of her.

"Not yet," Ashtin said.

"Relax," Kaden said. "You look tense when you should be happy. You're marrying a beautiful queen, and you'll soon be king of a prosperous planet."

Sten grunted. "All I want is Carys."

"We get it." Kaden gazed over to where Nea was chatting with some other knights. "Every day I wake up beside Nea and I'm grateful. She's everything. I'm fucking blessed."

"You and your Terran words," Ashtin said.

The knighthunter scoffed. "You use loads of Terran words. I think Kennedy is rubbing off on you in more ways than one."

Ashtin's face filled with pleasure. "I thank the knights every day that she came into my life." He looked at his lover as she crossed the room. She was talking with King Gayel of Eon and his Terran wife, Queen Alea.

"I feel like the three of us should thank the Gek'Dragar," Ashtin said. "Without them, we might never have ended up with our women."

Sten made a sound. "Let's not go too far."

The Gek'Dragar had been routed by the Oronis fleet and their allies. Sten had gotten word today that Ti-Lore had been freed, as had so many other worlds that the Gek'Dragar had invaded.

This time, they would monitor to ensure that the remaining Gek'Dragar didn't grow into a ravening army again.

There were gasps and people in the hall turned.

So did Sten, and everything inside him stilled.

Carys entered the ballroom. She wore a stunning gold dress that lovingly followed the lines of her slender body. It had touches of black and green. Silky dark fabric and gold chains draped out to the beaten metal bracelets on her wrists. It almost looked like she had wings.

Her platinum blonde hair was loose, and she wore her delicate black and gold crown on her head.

She looked stunning.

She was always beautiful to him. It didn't matter whether she was naked, laughing in bed, smiling at her people, or dressed in something magnificent like this.

She nodded and smiled at people, then her gaze lifted. When she saw him, a huge smile crossed her face.

Love swamped him. How had he gotten lucky enough to have this woman fall in love with him?

"Hello, my knightguard," she said.

"My queen."

"You look very handsome tonight." She smoothed a

hand across his shoulder. "And I have something for you." She gestured to one of her servers. The man hurried over, carrying an ornate wooden box. He opened the lid.

Sten saw what was inside and grimaced.

Carys was watching him, amusement on her face. "It's only a crown, Sten."

He made a non-committal sound. Thankfully, it wasn't overly large or ornate. It had a simple, masculine design and was made of black and gold metal to match hers.

She lifted it out of the box.

He knelt in front of her. "You're lucky that I'd do anything for you."

She settled the crown on his head, her lips curving. "I am." Then she raised her voice. "Rise, my consort." She leaned closer. "I love you."

"I love you too, Carys." He rose and pulled her into his arms.

She tipped her head back. "You've given me everything I've ever dreamed of, Sten."

He took her hand. Around them, everyone cheered and clapped. "Have I told you how stunning you look in that dress."

She shot him a private smile. "Thank you. And just so you know, I still feel you. Between my legs, from when you interrupted my bath earlier."

He fought back a shudder. Desire filled him, bright and hot.

"Now, shall we dance?" she asked.

"If we have to."

Her laughter sounded like gold. "It really is lucky that I know you'll do anything for me."

And he would.

He would be her king and consort. Her knightguard. He'd be her sword and shield, and always her devoted servant. But most of all, he would be the man who loved her for the rest of their lives.

EPILOGUE

Several years later

Carys stepped into the castle gardens.

The flowers were blooming, birds were chirping, and nearby, an *ashlan* tree was laden in red berries.

As she walked, the hem of her dress caught on the lush grass. Then the baby inside her kicked. Smiling, she rubbed a hand over her rather large belly. Her son was growing big, and he was already strong as evidenced by his fierce kicks. Strong, just like his father.

Giggles reached her. She looked across the garden and saw Sten with their daughter.

Everything inside Carys melted.

The little girl was the perfect blend of both of them. Callia had Carys' white-blonde hair but her father's green eyes. She was also stubborn, smart, and insatiably curious. She also adored her daddy.

Sten was an amazing father.

When they'd first discovered she was pregnant, he'd

been terrified. Then he'd been terrified again when the knighthealers had revealed she was having a girl. He hadn't been sure how to be a father to a little girl.

It turned out that he was brilliant. He doted on Callia, and, unsurprisingly, was a very protective father.

It reminded her that he'd once been worried about being king, too. But it turned out that he was brilliant at that as well.

They'd become partners. They backed each other, and their skills complemented each other. Carys always knew she could count on his strength and support, no matter what.

She looked past her husband and daughter, and smiled at the shining city beyond. Her parents would be proud.

She heard more laughter. An older boy ran across the grass to Sten and Callia.

Sten ruffled the boy's hair. Eve and Davion's son Kane was growing tall and strong. He tossed a ball at Callia. The little girl tried to catch it but missed, giggling wildly.

Patiently, Kane retrieved the ball and threw it again.

"He's such a good boy." Eve stepped up beside Carys. "He doesn't get his patience from me."

"I'm just wondering how long it will take him to work out that Callia can catch the ball just fine. She's playing him."

Eve laughed. "Clever girl. Keeping them on their toes already."

Eve, Davion, and Kane were currently visiting Oron

for several days. The ties between the Oronis and the Eon had only grown stronger with time.

As they had with Earth.

On a blanket under the trees, Kennedy sat eating some of the *ashlan* berries. Ashtin had married his Terran, and Kennedy had become one of Carys' closest friends.

Kennedy's pregnancy wasn't showing yet, but that didn't stop Ashtin from hovering. It was making him even more overprotective than usual. He stood talking with Davion, but Carys knew his full attention was on his wife.

He was driving Kennedy crazy, but Kennedy was managing him well.

Carys smiled. She was surrounded by friends and family. And peace. Peace on her planet, in the quadrant, among their allies.

There were still skirmishes at the borders, but at least the surviving Gek'Dragar remained on their homeworld. They were rebuilding their leadership, and had vowed to be different.

"Callia's like Sten," Carys said. "Watchful and stubborn."

"I don't know," Eve said. "I hear the knightqueen of the Oronis can be stubborn when she wants to be."

Carys laughed and slapped Eve's arm.

"Mally!" Callia called out, rushing across the grass.

A tall boy with deep-red skin and long black hair had entered the garden. Malthor was taller than Carys now, and had turned into part boy, part man. He was staying with them while he studied engineering in the city before he returned to Ti-Lore.

Azulon, Nythoria, and the others were working hard to rebuild their world. They'd made strong partnerships with not only the Oronis, but other worlds as well.

They were forming an alliance with worlds close to Gek'Dragar space. A coalition that would ensure they had the strength to stand against any enemy.

Malthor lifted Callia up and propped her on his hip. Then he turned to speak with Sten. No doubt to schedule more training. Sten was teaching the young man to use a sword.

Yes, Carys was happy.

Truly happy.

The only people missing were Nea and Kaden. The couple were currently off on an exploration mission to the Darmiss quadrant. They both loved nothing more than being off on a new adventure.

"While Kane is busy kicking that ball, I'm going to sneak into the garden with my man for a minute alone." Eve winked, and then headed toward her mate.

When Carys looked up, Sten was walking toward her.

He had more gray in his hair now, and his face was more rugged. She loved it.

He wrapped his arms around her, one large hand resting on her belly.

"How can I love you more each day, my knightking?" she asked.

"Because I'm yours." He dropped a kiss to her lips. "Always yours. Anything you command, I'll do for you."

"That might be it," she murmured.

"How is our son this morning?"

"Busy as always."

"You should rest when Callia has her nap."

Carys nuzzled his chest. "Only if you join me."

"I'm scheduled to do some training with the new knightguards." He still spent time training and working with the knights.

She arched a brow.

"But I can postpone that," he said.

"Good."

He cupped the side of her face, thumb rubbing her skin. "I am Knightking Thorsten. It is my duty to protect my queen. I am her sword, her shield, and her devoted king and husband. And I will love you as long as I have breath in my body."

Her heart melted at the familiar words he told her often. "*Sten.*"

He lifted a hand and waved at their nanny, who stood at the edge of the garden. "See that Callia goes down for her nap. I'm escorting the knightqueen to her quarters. She needs her rest."

The nanny nodded and smiled, her gaze returning to their little girl.

Then Sten scooped Carys into his arms. She slid her hand across his broad shoulders as he carried her inside the castle.

She nibbled at his ear. "Are we really going to rest?"

"Yes. After I ensure that you're too tired to do anything else. It's my duty, after all."

Stars, she loved him. Her delighted laughter echoed in the hall as they headed for their quarters.

I hope you enjoyed Carys and Sten's story, and the end of the Oronis Knights trilogy!

Want to find out more about the Eon Warriors? Check out the first book in the **Eon Warriors**, *Edge of Eon*. **Read on for a preview of the first chapter.**

Don't miss out! For updates about new releases, free books, and other fun stuff, sign up for my VIP mailing list and get your *free box set* containing three action-packed romances.

Visit here to get started: www.annahackett.com

KNIGHTQUEEN

Would you like a FREE BOX SET of my books?

PREVIEW: EDGE OF EON

She shifted on the chair, causing the chains binding her hands to clank together. Eve Traynor snorted. The wrist and ankle restraints were overkill. She was on a low-orbit prison circling

Earth. Where the fuck did they think she was going to go?

Eve shifted her shoulders to try to ease the tension from having her hands tied behind her back. For the millionth time, she studied her surroundings. The medium-sized room was empty, except for her chair. Everything from the floor to the ceiling was dull-gray metal. All of the Citadel Prison was drab and sparse. She'd learned every boring inch of it the last few months.

One wide window provided the only break in the otherwise uniform space. Outside, she caught a tantalizing glimpse of the blue-green orb of Earth below.

Her gut clenched and she drank in the sight of her home. Five months she'd been locked away in this prison. Five months since her life had imploded.

She automatically thought of her sisters. She sucked in a deep breath. She hated everything they'd had to go through because of what had happened. Hell, she thought of her mom as well, even though their last contact had been the day after Eve had been imprisoned. Her mom had left Eve a drunken, scathing message.

The door to the room opened, and Eve lifted her chin and braced.

When she saw the dark-blue Space Corps uniform, she stiffened. When she saw the row of stars on the lapel, she gritted her teeth.

Admiral Linda Barber stepped into the room, accompanied by a female prison guard. The admiral's hair was its usual sleek bob of highlighted, ash-blonde hair. Her brown eyes were steady.

Eve looked at the guard. "Take me back to my cell."

The admiral lifted a hand. "Please leave us."

The guard hesitated. "That's against protocol, ma'am—"

"It'll be fine." The admiral's stern voice said she was giving an order, not making a request.

The guard hesitated again, then ducked through the door. It clicked closed behind her.

Eve sniffed. "Say what you have to say and leave."

Admiral Barber sighed, taking a few steps closer. "I know you're angry. You have a right to be—"

"You think?" Eve sucked back the rush of molten anger. "I got tossed under the fucking starship to save a mama's boy. A mama's boy who had no right to be in command of one of Space Corps' vessels."

Shit. Eve wanted to pummel something. Preferably the face of Robert J. Hathaway—golden son of Rear-Admiral Elisabeth Hathaway. A man who, because of family connections, was given captaincy of the *Orion*, even though he lacked the intelligence and experience needed to lead it.

Meanwhile, Eve—a Space Corps veteran—had worked her ass off during her career in the Corps, and had been promised her own ship, only to be denied her chance. Instead, she'd been assigned as Hathaway's second-in-command. To be a glorified babysitter, and to actually run the ship, just without the title and the pay raise.

She'd swallowed it. Swallowed Hathaway's incompetence and blowhard bullshit. Until he'd fucked up. Big-time.

"The Haumea Incident was regrettable," Barber said.

Eve snorted. "Mostly for the people who died. And definitely for me, since I'm the one shackled to a chair in the Citadel. Meanwhile, I assume Bobby Hathaway is still a dedicated Space Corps employee."

"He's no longer a captain of a ship. And he never will be again."

"Right. Mommy got him a cushy desk job back at Space Corps Headquarters."

The silence was deafening and it made Eve want to kick something.

"I'm sorry, Eve. We all know what happened wasn't right."

Eve jerked on her chains and they clanked against the chair. "And you let it happen. All of Space Corps leadership did, to appease Mommy Hathaway. I dedicated my life to the Corps, and you all screwed me over for an admiral's incompetent son. I got sentenced to prison for *his* mistakes." Stomach turning in vicious circles, Eve looked at the floor, sucking in air. She stared at the soft booties on her feet. Damned inmate footwear. She wasn't even allowed proper fucking shoes.

Admiral Barber moved to her side. "I'm here to offer you a chance at freedom."

Gaze narrowing, Eve looked up. Barber looked... nervous. Eve had never seen the self-assured woman nervous before.

"There's a mission. If you complete it, you'll be released from prison."

Interesting. "And reinstated? With a full pardon?"

Barber's lips pursed and her face looked pinched. "We can negotiate."

So, no. "Screw your offer." Eve would prefer to rot in her cell, rather than help the Space Corps.

The admiral moved in front of her, her low-heeled pumps echoing on the floor. "Eve, the fate of the world depends on this mission."

Barber's serious tone sent a shiver skating down Eve's spine. She met the woman's brown eyes.

"The Kantos are gathering their forces just beyond the boundary at Station Omega V."

Fuck. The Kantos. The insectoid alien race had been nipping at Earth for years. Their humanoid-insectoid soldiers were the brains of the operation, but they encompassed all manner of ugly, insect-like beasts as well.

With the invention of zero-point drives several decades ago, Earth's abilities for space exploration had exploded. Then, thirty years ago, they'd made first contact with an alien species—the Eon.

The Eon shared a common ancestor with the humans of Earth. They were bigger and broader, with a few differing organs, but generally human-looking. They had larger lungs, a stronger, bigger heart, and a more efficiently-designed digestion system. This gave them increased strength and stamina, which in turn made them excellent warriors. Unfortunately, they also wanted nothing to do with Earth and its inferior Terrans.

The Eon, and their fearsome warriors and warships, stayed inside their own space and had banned Terrans from crossing their boundaries.

Then, twenty years ago, the first unfortunate and bloody meeting with the Kantos had occurred.

Since then, the Kantos had returned repeatedly to

nip at the Terran borders—attacking ships, space stations, and colonies.

But it had become obvious in the last year or so that the Kantos had something bigger planned. The Haumea Incident had made that crystal clear.

The Kantos wanted Earth. There were to be no treaties, alliances, or negotiations. They wanted to descend like locusts and decimate everything—all the planet's resources, and most of all, the humans.

Yes, the Kantos wanted to freaking use humans as a food source. Eve suppressed a shudder.

"And?" she said.

"We have to do whatever it takes to save our planet."

Eve tilted her head. "The Eon."

Admiral Barber smiled. "You were always sharp, Eve. Yes, the Eon are the only ones with the numbers, the technology, and the capability to help us repel the Kantos."

"Except they want nothing to do with us." No one had seen or spoken with an Eon for three decades.

"Desperate times call for desperate measures."

Okay, Eve felt that shiver again. She felt like she was standing on the edge of a platform, about to be shoved under the starship again.

"What's the mission?" she asked carefully.

"We want you to abduct War Commander Davion Thann-Eon."

Holy fuck. Eve's chest clenched so tight she couldn't even draw a breath. Then the air rushed into her lungs, and she threw her head back and laughed. Tears ran down her face.

"You're kidding."

But the admiral wasn't laughing.

Eve shook her head. "That's a fucking suicide mission. You want me to abduct the deadliest, most decorated Eon war commander who controls the largest, most destructive Eon warship in their fleet?"

"Yes."

"No."

"Eve, you have a record of making...risky decisions."

Eve shook her head. "I always calculate the risks."

"Yes, but you use a higher margin of error than the rest of us."

"I've always completed my missions successfully." The Haumea Incident excluded, since that was Bobby's brilliant screw-up.

"Yes. That's why we know if anyone has a chance of making this mission a success, it's you."

"I may as well take out a blaster and shoot myself right now. One, I'll never make it into Eon space, let alone aboard the *Desteron*."

Since the initial encounter, they'd collected whatever intel they could on the Eon. Eve had seen secret schematics of that warship. And she had to admit, the thought of being aboard that ship left her a little damp between her thighs. She loved space and flying, and the big, sleek warship was something straight out of her fantasies.

"We have an experimental, top-of-the-line stealth ship for you to use," the admiral said.

Eve carried on like the woman hadn't spoken. "And two, even if I got close to the war commander, he's bigger and stronger than me, not to mention bonded to a fucking deadly alien symbiont that gives him added strength and the ability to create organic armor and weapons with a single thought. I'd be dead in seconds."

"We recovered a…substance that is able to contain the symbiont the Eon use."

Eve narrowed her eyes. "Recovered from where?"

Admiral Barber cleared her throat. "From the wreck of a Kantos ship. It was clearly tech they were developing to use against the Eon."

Shit. "So I'm to abduct the war commander, and then further enrage him by neutralizing his symbiont."

"We believe the containment is temporary, and there is an antidote."

Eve shook her head. "This is beyond insane."

"For the fate of humanity, we have to try."

"*Talk* to them," Eve said. "Use some diplomacy."

"We tried. They refused all contact."

Because humans were simply ants to the Eon. Small, insignificant, an annoyance.

Although, truth be told, humanity only had itself to blame. By all accounts, Terrans hadn't behaved very well at first contact. The meetings with the Eon had turned into blustering threats, different countries trying to make alliances with the aliens while happily stabbing each other in the back.

Now Earth wanted to abduct an Eon war commander. No, not a war commander, *the* war commander. So dumb. She wished she had a hand free so she could slap it over her eyes.

"Find another sacrificial lamb."

The admiral was silent for a long moment. "If you won't do it for yourself or for humanity, then do it for your sisters."

Eve's blood chilled and she cocked her head. "What's this got to do with my sisters?"

"They've made a lot of noise about your imprisonment. Agitating for your freedom."

Eve breathed through her nose. God, she loved her sisters. Still, she didn't know whether to be pleased or pissed. "And?"

"Your sister has shared some classified information with the press about the Haumea Incident."

Eve fought back a laugh. Lara wasn't shy about sharing her thoughts about this entire screwed-up situation. Eve's older sister was a badass Space Corps special forces marine. Lara wouldn't hesitate to take down anyone who pissed her off, the Space Corps included.

"And she had access to information she should not have had access to, meaning your other sister has done some...creative hacking."

Dammit. The rush of love was mixed with some annoyance. Sweet, geeky Wren had a giant, super-smart brain. She was a computer-systems engineer for some company with cutting-edge technology in Japan. It helped keep her baby sister's big brain busy, because Wren hadn't found a computer she couldn't hack.

"Plenty of people are unhappy with what your sisters have been stirring up," Barber continued.

Eve stiffened. She didn't like where this was going.

"I've tried to run interference—"

"Admiral—"

Barber held up a hand. "I can't keep protecting them, Eve. I've been trying, but some of this is even above my pay grade. If you don't do this mission, powers outside of my control will go after them. They'll both end up in a cell right alongside yours until the Kantos arrive and blow this prison out of the sky."

Her jaw tight, Eve's brain turned all the information over. *Fucking fuck.*

"Eve, if there is anyone who has a chance of succeeding on this mission, it's you."

Eve stayed silent.

Barber stepped closer. "I don't care if you do it for yourself, the billions of people of Earth, or your sisters—"

"I'll do it." The words shot out of Eve, harsh and angry.

She'd do it—abduct the scariest alien war commander in the galaxy—for all the reasons the admiral listed—to clear her name, for her freedom, to save the world, and for the sisters she loved.

Honestly, it didn't matter anyway, because the odds of her succeeding and coming back alive were zero.

EVE LEFT THE STARSHIP GYM, towel around her neck, and her muscles warm and limber from her workout.

God, it was nice to work out when it suited her. On the Citadel Prison, exercise time was strictly scheduled, monitored, and timed.

Two crew members came into view, heading down

the hall toward her. As soon as the uniformed men spotted her, they looked at the floor and passed her quickly.

Eve rolled her eyes. Well, she wasn't aboard the *Polaris* to make friends, and she had to admit, she had a pretty notorious reputation. She'd never been one to blindly follow the rules, plus there was the Haumea Incident and her imprisonment. And her family were infamous in the Space Corps. Her father had been a space marine, killed in action in one of the early Kantos encounters. Her mom had been a decorated Space Corps member, but after Eve's dad had died, her mom had started drinking. It had deteriorated until she'd gone off the rails. She'd done it quite publicly, blaming the Space Corps for her husband's death. In the process, she'd forgotten she had three young, grieving girls.

Yep, Eve was well aware that the people you cared for most either left you, or let you down. The employer you worked your ass off for treated you like shit. The only two people in the galaxy that didn't apply to were her sisters.

Eve pushed thoughts of her parents away. Instead, she scanned the starship. The *Polaris* was a good ship. A mid-size cruiser, she was designed for exploration, but well-armed as well. Eve guessed they'd be heading out beyond Neptune about now.

The plan was for the *Polaris* to take her to the edge of Eon space, where she'd take a tiny, two-person stealth ship, sneak up to the *Desteron*, then steal onboard.

Piece of cake. She rolled her eyes.

Back in her small cabin, she took a quick shower,

dressed, and then headed to the ops room. It was a small room close to the bridge that the ship's captain had made available to her.

She stepped inside, and all the screens flickered to life. A light table stood in the center of the room, and everything was filled with every scrap of intel that the Space Corps had on the Eon Empire, their warriors, the *Desteron*, and War Commander Thann-Eon.

It was more than she'd guessed. A lot of it had been classified. There was fascinating intel on the four Eon homeworld planets—Eon, Jad, Felis, and Ath. Each Eon warrior carried their homeworld in their name, along with their clan names. The war commander hailed from the planet Eon, and Thann was a clan known as a warrior clan.

Eve swiped her fingers across the light table and studied pictures of the *Desteron*. They were a few years old and taken from a great distance, but that didn't hide the warship's power.

It was fearsome. Black, sleek, and impressive. It was built for speed and stealth, but also power. It had to be packed with weapons beyond their imagination.

She touched the screen again and slid the image to the side. Another image appeared—the only known picture of War Commander Thann-Eon.

Jesus. The man packed a punch. All Eon warriors looked alike—big, broad-shouldered, muscular. They all had longish hair—not quite reaching the shoulders, but not cut short, either. Their hair usually ranged from dark brown to a tawny, golden-brown. There was no black or blond hair among the Eon. Their skin color ranged from dark-brown to light-brown, as well.

Before first contact had gone sour, both sides had done some DNA testing, and confirmed the Eon and Terrans shared an ancestor.

The war commander was wearing a pitch-black, sleeveless uniform. He was tall, built, with long legs and powerful thighs. He was exactly the kind of man you expected to stride onto a battlefield, pull a sword, and slaughter everyone. He had a strong face, one that shouted power. Eve stroked a finger over the image. He had a square jaw, a straight, almost aggressive nose, and a well-formed brow. His eyes were as dark as space, but shot through with intriguing threads of blue.

"It's you and me, War Commander." If he didn't kill her, first.

Suddenly, sirens blared.

Eve didn't stop to think. She slammed out of the ops room and sprinted onto the bridge.

Inside, the large room was a flurry of activity.

Captain Chen stood in the center of the space, barking orders at his crew.

Her heart contracted. God, she'd missed this so much. The vibration of the ship beneath her feet, her team around her, even the scent of recycled starship air.

"You shouldn't be in here," a sharp voice snapped.

Eve turned, locking gazes with the stocky, bearded XO. Sub-Captain Porter wasn't a fan of hers.

"Leave her," Captain Chen told his second-in-command. "She's seen more Kantos ships than all of us combined."

The captain looked back at his team. "Shields up."

Eve studied the screen and the Kantos ship approaching.

It looked like a bug. It had large, outstretched legs, and a bulky, segmented, central fuselage. It wasn't the biggest ship she'd seen, but it wasn't small, either. It was probably out on some intel mission.

"Sir," a female voice called out. "We're getting a distress call from the *Panama*, a cargo ship en route to Nightingale Space Station. They're under attack from a swarm of small Kantos ships."

Eve sucked in a breath, her hand curling into a fist. This was a usual Kantos tactic. They would overwhelm a ship with their small swarm ships. It had ugly memories of the Haumea Incident stabbing at her.

"Open the comms channel," the captain ordered.

"Please...help us." A harried man's voice came over the distorted comm line. "...can't hold out much...thirty-seven crew onboard...we are..."

Suddenly, a huge explosion of light flared in the distance.

Eve's shoulders sagged. The cargo ship was gone.

"Goddammit," the XO bit out.

The front legs of the larger Kantos ship in front of them started to glow orange.

"They're going to fire," Eve said.

The captain straightened. "Evasive maneuvers."

His crew raced to obey the orders, the *Polaris* veering suddenly to the right.

"The swarm ships will be on their way back." Eve knew the Kantos loved to swarm like locusts.

"Release the tridents," the captain said.

Good. Eve watched the small, triple-pronged space mines rain out the side of the ship. They'd be a dangerous minefield for the Kantos swarm.

The main Kantos ship swung around.

"They're locking weapons," someone shouted.

Eve fought the need to shout out orders and offer the captain advice. Last time she'd done that, she'd ended up in shackles.

The blast hit the *Polaris*, the shields lighting up from the impact. The ship shuddered.

"Shields holding, but depleting," another crew member called out.

"Sub-Captain Traynor?" The captain's dark gaze met hers.

Something loosened in her chest. "It's a raider-class cruiser, Captain. You're smaller and more maneuverable. You need to circle around it, spray it with laser fire. Its weak spots are on the sides. Sustained laser fire will eventually tear it open. You also need to avoid the legs."

"Fly circles around it?" a young man at a console said. "That's crazy."

Eve eyed the lead pilot. "You up for this?"

The man swallowed. "I don't think I can..."

"Sure you can, if you want us to survive this."

"Walker, do it," the captain barked.

The pilot pulled in a breath and the *Polaris* surged forward. They rounded the Kantos ship. Up close, the bronze-brown hull looked just like the carapace of an insect. One of the legs swung up, but Walker had quick reflexes.

"Fire," Eve said.

The weapons officer started firing. Laser fire hit the Kantos ship in a pretty row of orange.

"Keep going," Eve urged.

They circled the ship, firing non-stop.

Eve crossed her arms over her chest. Everything in her was still, but alive, filled with energy. She'd always known she was born to stand on the bridge of a starship.

"More," she urged. "Keep firing."

"Swarm ships incoming," a crew member yelled.

"Hold," Eve said calmly. "Trust the mines." She eyed the perspiring weapons officer. "What's your name, Lieutenant?"

"Law, ma'am. Lieutenant Miriam Law."

"You're doing fine, Law. Ignore the swarm ships and keep firing on the cruiser."

The swarm ships rushed closer, then hit the field of mines. Eve saw the explosions, like brightly colored pops of fireworks.

The lasers kept cutting into the hull of the larger Kantos ship. She watched the ship's engines fire. They were going to try and make a run for it.

"Bring us around, Walker. Fire everything you have, Law."

They swung around to face the side of the Kantos ship straight on. The laser ripped into the hull.

There was a blinding flash of light, and startled exclamations filled the bridge. She squinted until the light faded away.

On the screen, the Kantos ship broke up into pieces.

Captain Chen released a breath. "Thank you, Sub-Captain."

Eve inclined her head. She glanced at the silent crew. "Good flying, Walker. And excellent shooting, Law."

But she looked back at the screen, at the debris hanging in space and the last of the swarm ships retreating.

They'd keep coming. No matter what. It was ingrained in the Kantos to destroy.

They had to be stopped.

Eon Warriors
Edge of Eon
Touch of Eon
Heart of Eon
Kiss of Eon
Mark of Eon
Claim of Eon
Storm of Eon
Soul of Eon
King of Eon
Also Available as Audiobooks!

PREVIEW: GALACTIC KINGS

Want more action-packed sci-fi romance? Then check out the **Galactic Kings**.

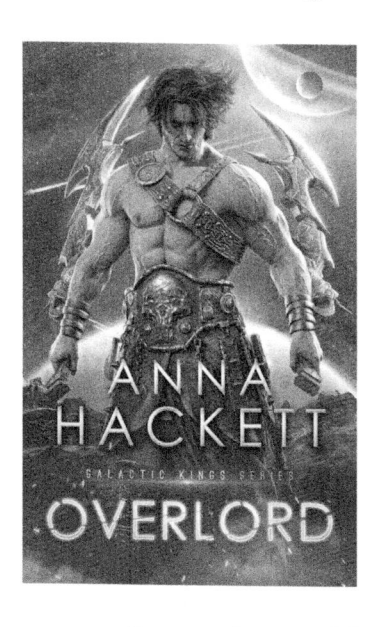

When an experimental starship test goes

horribly wrong, a test pilot from Earth is flung across the galaxy and crash lands on the planet of a powerful alien king.

Pilot Mallory West is having a really bad day. She's crashed on an alien planet, her ship is in pieces, and her best friend Poppy, the scientist monitoring the experiment, is missing. Dazed and injured, she collapses into the arms of a big, silver-eyed warrior king. But when her rescuer cuffs her to a bed and accuses her of being a spy, Mal knows she has to escape her darkly tempting captor and find her friend.

Overlord Rhain Zhalto Sarkany is in a battle to protect his planet Zhalto and his people from his evil, power-hungry father. He'll use every one of his deadly Zhalton abilities to win the fight against his father's lethal warlord and army of vicious creatures. Rhain suspects the tough, intriguing woman he pulls from a starship wreck is a trap, but when Mal escapes, he is compelled to track her down.

Fighting their overwhelming attraction, Mal and Rhain join forces to hunt down the warlord and find Poppy. But as Mal's body reacts to Zhalto's environment, it awakens dormant powers, and Rhain is the only one who can help her. As the warlord launches a brutal attack, it will take all of Mal and Rhain's combined powers to save their friends, the planet, and themselves.

Galactic Kings
Overlord

KNIGHTQUEEN

Emperor
Captain of the Guard
Conqueror
Also Available as Audiobooks!

ALSO BY ANNA HACKETT

Fury Brothers

Fury

Keep

Burn

Also Available as Audiobooks!

Unbroken Heroes

The Hero She Needs

The Hero She Wants

Also Available as Audiobooks!

Sentinel Security

Wolf

Hades

Striker

Steel

Excalibur

Hex

Also Available as Audiobooks!

Norcross Security

The Investigator

The Troubleshooter

The Specialist

The Bodyguard

The Hacker

The Powerbroker

The Detective

The Medic

The Protector

Also Available as Audiobooks!

Billionaire Heists

Stealing from Mr. Rich

Blackmailing Mr. Bossman

Hacking Mr. CEO

Also Available as Audiobooks!

Team 52

Mission: Her Protection

Mission: Her Rescue

Mission: Her Security

Mission: Her Defense

Mission: Her Safety

Mission: Her Freedom

Mission: Her Shield

Mission: Her Justice

Also Available as Audiobooks!

Treasure Hunter Security

Undiscovered

Uncharted

Unexplored

Unfathomed

Untraveled

Unmapped

Unidentified

Undetected

Also Available as Audiobooks!

Oronis Knights

Knightmaster

Knighthunter

Galactic Kings

Overlord

Emperor

Captain of the Guard

Conqueror

Also Available as Audiobooks!

Eon Warriors

Edge of Eon

Touch of Eon

Heart of Eon

Kiss of Eon

Mark of Eon

Claim of Eon

Storm of Eon

Soul of Eon

King of Eon

Also Available as Audiobooks!

Galactic Gladiators: House of Rone

Sentinel

Defender

Centurion

Paladin

Guard

Weapons Master

Also Available as Audiobooks!

Galactic Gladiators

Gladiator

Warrior

Hero

Protector

Champion

Barbarian

Beast

Rogue

Guardian

Cyborg

Imperator

Hunter

Also Available as Audiobooks!

Hell Squad

Marcus

Cruz

Gabe

Reed

Roth

Noah

Shaw

Holmes

Niko

Finn

Devlin

Theron

Hemi

Ash

Levi

Manu

Griff

Dom

Survivors

Tane

Also Available as Audiobooks!

The Anomaly Series

Time Thief

Mind Raider

Soul Stealer

Salvation

Anomaly Series Box Set

The Phoenix Adventures

Among Galactic Ruins

At Star's End

In the Devil's Nebula

On a Rogue Planet

Beneath a Trojan Moon

Beyond Galaxy's Edge

On a Cyborg Planet

Return to Dark Earth

On a Barbarian World

Lost in Barbarian Space

Through Uncharted Space

Crashed on an Ice World

Perma Series

Winter Fusion

A Galactic Holiday

Warriors of the Wind

Tempest

Storm & Seduction

Fury & Darkness

Standalone Titles

Savage Dragon

Hunter's Surrender

One Night with the Wolf

For more information visit www.annahackett.com

ABOUT THE AUTHOR

I'm a USA Today bestselling romance author who's passionate about **_fast-paced, emotion-filled_** contemporary romantic suspense and science fiction romance. I love writing about people overcoming unbeatable odds and achieving seemingly impossible goals. I like to believe it's possible for all of us to do the same.

I live in Australia with my own personal hero and two very busy, always-on-the-move sons.

For release dates, behind-the-scenes info, free books, and other fun stuff, sign up for the latest news here:

Website: www.annahackett.com

Printed in Great Britain
by Amazon

45818465R00148